D0031428

Dear Mr. President™

OTHER DEAR MR. PRESIDENT™ BOOKS

Thomas Jefferson
Letters from a Philadelphia Bookworm
By Jennifer Armstrong

Theodore Roosevelt
Letters from a Young Coal Miner
By Jennifer Armstrong

Abraham Lincoln
Letters from a Slave Girl
by Andrea Davis Pinkney

John Quincy Adams
Letters from a Southern Planter's Son
by Steven Kroll

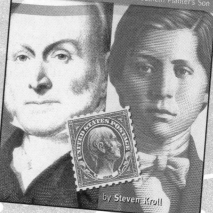

READ YOUR WAY INTO THE PAST...

History comes alive in this collection of fictitious letters exchanged between President Franklin D. Roosevelt and mill-town girl Emma Bartoletti. But there is much more to discover.

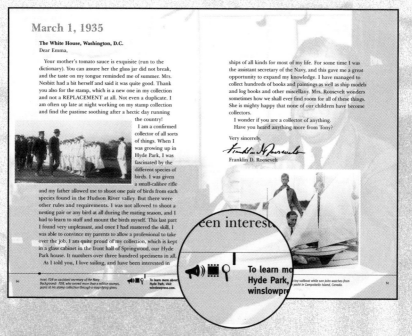

Throughout the book, there is a series of "interactive footnotes" called Web prompts leading the reader to our virtual library at **winslowpress.com**. Once there they will find out more about many of the topics discussed in the letters of the book as well as links for further exploration, pictures, and even audio and video clips.

Icons next to each footnote in the book let readers know what kinds of additional resources they will find when they visit the Web site.

PHOTOGRAPHS

VIDEO CLIPS

AUDIO CLIPS

LINKS

CLICK TO MAKE IT COME ALIVE AT WINSLOWPRESS.COM

VISIT THE DEAR MR. PRESIDENT WEB SITE AT WINSLOWPRESS.COM

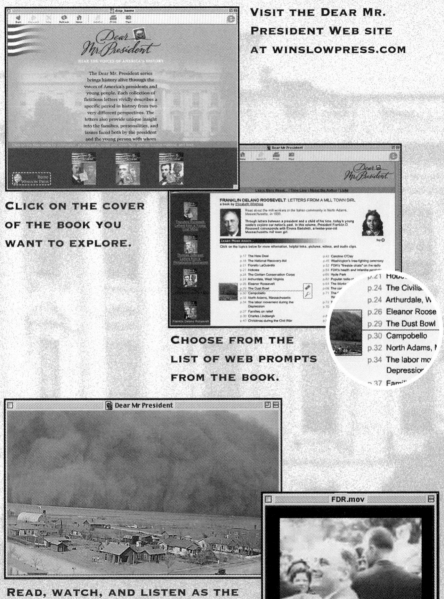

CLICK ON THE COVER OF THE BOOK YOU WANT TO EXPLORE.

CHOOSE FROM THE LIST OF WEB PROMPTS FROM THE BOOK.

READ, WATCH, AND LISTEN AS THE TOPICS UNFOLD BEFORE YOUR EYES.

Dear Mr. President ™

Franklin D. Roosevelt
Letters from a Mill Town Girl

by Elizabeth Winthrop

WINSLOW PRESS

New York

Discover *Dear Mr. President*'s™ interactive Web site with worldwide
links, games, activities, and more at **winslowpress.com**

Acknowledgments:

In researching a project of this scope and detail, I relied on a number of people who provided me with actual facts and dates and many others who amplified my understanding of the historical era as well as the specifics of the town of North Adams through stories and anecdotes. Some people asked not to be acknowledged publicly, so I express my gratitude to them here anonymously. The others include: Marion Grillon, Jill Laurello, Kim DiLego, Robin Martin, Marcia Gross, and the rest of the helpful staff at the North Adams Public Library; Deborah Sprague, Lorraine Maloney, and Robert Campanile of the North Adams Historical Society for their support and patience as I tracked down detail after detail of North Adams during the Great Depression; Mark Rondeau of the *Advocate* for information on Italian immigration and Babe Ruth's visit to North Adams; Kathleen Reilly, supervisor of the Local History Department at the Berkshire Athenaeum, Pittsfield, Massachusetts, for help with researching the naturalization process and the Civilian Conservation Corps camps in the Berkshire Hills.

For their memories of North Adams during the Depression, I am very grateful to Tony Talarico, Rosalie Cancro Morgan, Roger Rivers, Josephine Campedelli, Venice Partenope, Henry Puppolo, and the North Adams Sons of Italy Lodge #704. For a greater understanding of labor conditions and social history in North Adams during the 30s and 40s, I thank Maynard Seider and Paul W. Marino. Thanks also to Joe Manning for welcoming me to North Adams with stories, for setting me straight when I went off course, and for those writerly chats at the Bean. I am grateful to Mindy Hackner and the rest of the tireless staff of the David and Joyce Milne Public Library in Williamstown. Thanks to Dylan and Jocelyn at the Cold Spring Roasters Coffee Shop, who always remembered the almond syrup, and to Robin and Lorie at Lickety Split, who fed me soup and company during lunch hour.

A special thanks to researchers Irene Connelly and Sheri Bunn, who answered my barrage of questions promptly and in great detail.

Winslow Press wishes to acknowledge the following sources for the photographs and illustrations used in this book: The Library of Congress, The North Adams Historical Society and The Franklin D. Roosevelt Library.

Thanks to R. Sean Wilentz, Dayton-Stockton Professor of History, and Director, Program in American Studies, Princeton University, for evaluating the manuscript.

DEAR MR. PRESIDENT ™ and the DEAR MR. PRESIDENT ™ logo are registered trademarks of Winslow Press.

Library of Congress Cataloging-in-Publication Data
Winthrop, Elizabeth.
Franklin D. Roosevelt: letters from a mill town girl / by Elizabeth Winthrop.
p. cm.
Includes biographical references and indexes.
Summary: Between 1933 and 1935, a young Italian American girl living in North Adams, Massachusetts, corresponds with President Franklin Roosevelt about the conditions in her town, Mr. Roosevelt's New Deal programs, and her own family's activities.
ISBN: 1-890817-61-9
1. Roosevelt, Franklin D. (Franklin Delano), 1882-1945—Juvenile Fiction [1. Roosevelt, Franklin D. (Franklin Delano), 1882-1945—Fiction. 2. Depressions-1929—Fiction. 3. Italian Americans—Fiction. 4. Letters—Fiction.] I. Title. II. Series.

PZ7.W768 Fr 2001
[Fic]-dc21
2001020260

Creative Director: Bretton Clark

Book
Designer: Victoria Stehl
Editor: Margery Cuyler
Cover illustration: Mark Summers

Web site
Designer: Patricia Espinosa
Programmer: John Fontana
Editor: Laura Harris

Printed in Belgium
First edition, October 2001
2 4 6 8 10 9 7 5 3 1

WINSLOW PRESS

115 East 23RD Street 10TH Floor
New York, NY 10010

Discover *Dear Mr. President's* ™ interactive Web site with worldwide links, games, activities, and more at **winslowpress.com**

In memoriam

Jessie Bartoletti
1911-1999

and to the people of
North Adams, generous
storytellers and preservers
of history

A Note from the Publisher

This book is our fourth in the *Dear Mr. President* ™ series. The text is in the form of letters—in this book, letters exchanged between President Franklin D. Roosevelt and a twelve-year-old girl, Emma Bartoletti. Although the letters are fictional, the information in them is based on meticulous research. In order to capture President Roosevelt's personality and the voice of the youth of the time as well as gather facts about the Depression, the author relied on such books as *No Ordinary Time* by Doris Kearns Goodwin and *FDR, 1882–1945* by Joseph Alsop.

To find out firsthand about life in a Massachusetts mill town in 1933–1937, the author conducted extensive interviews with the citizens of North Adams who lived through it. A list of recommended reading can be found on pages 130-131.

It is our hope that the *Dear Mr. President* ™ books and their portrayal of issues from other times will provide readers with valuable insights into important moments of American history. Each title, written by a skilled author, is further enhanced by interactive footnotes, games, activities, and links, plus detailed historical information, at the book's own home page in our virtual library, winslowpress.com.

By offering you a rich reading experience coupled with our interactive Web site, we encourage you to embrace the future with what's best from the past.

Diane F. Kessenich, Publisher and CEO, Winslow Press

The man standing in the doorway worked for twelve years as a coal loader in Scotts Run, West Virginia, before losing his job, c. 1933.

Dear Mr. President,

Your Friend,

Emma Bartoletti

Dear Miss Emma Bartoletti,

Very Sincerely Yours,

In the early 1930s, America was in big trouble. One quarter of the workforce had no work. Banks in thirty-eight states had closed, and many others were on the brink of collapse. Two hundred thousand teenagers had joined desperate adults who were riding the trains from one town to another, searching for work that didn't exist. Whole families thrown out of their homes were living in makeshift shacks in the city parks and on the edges of small American towns. They named these shantytowns "Hoovervilles" after President Herbert Hoover, who seemed to be doing nothing to make things better.

On November 8, 1932, the country elected a new president, a Democrat named Franklin Delano Roosevelt. Here was a man who spoke directly to the forgotten people of America. He told them that the only thing they had to fear was fear itself. He told them that he knew they wanted action, and he would give them action. He promised them a New Deal. Millions of the listeners who gathered around radios to hear his "fireside chats" felt that he was speaking directly to each one of them. They called him FDR, and they believed that he understood their troubles. They trusted him. They claimed him as their champion.

The Depression touched every corner of the country. In New England, many immigrants worked long hours in dusty rooms in cotton mills under the incessant clatter of machinery. There were no lunch hours, no sick days, and no vacations, but the textile workers didn't dare complain. As long as the mills stayed open, they would have a job. They wouldn't be thrown out of their homes. They wouldn't have to go on the dole.

The children of the Great Depression were caught up in their families' struggles. They knew better than children of later generations how much a loaf of bread cost and how far a dollar would go. President Roosevelt and his wife, Eleanor, received five to eight thousand letters a day. Most of these came from everyday working people who had lost jobs and homes. Many of their children took turns eating or going to school because there wasn't enough food or they had to share one pair of shoes. Many of the president's letters came from the children themselves.

Imagine, then, a girl named Emma Bartoletti living in the mill town of North Adams, Massachusetts, during the Depression. Emma would have been educated in American public schools and would have spoken English better than her Italian immigrant parents. She would have listened to the radio and read the newspapers. She would have had many things to say to this new president about her life in a New England factory town. And she would have had questions to ask him. Imagine Emma writing to Franklin Delano Roosevelt, the thirty-second president of the United States of America, in September 1933.

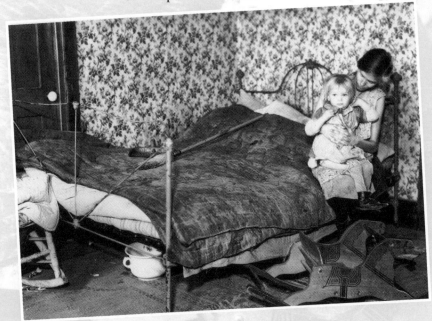

The Depression was hard on this pregnant mother, weakened by tuberculosis and poverty.

To learn more about the New Deal, visit winslowpress.com.

19

SIMMS LIBRARY
ALBUQUERQUE ACADEMY

North Adams, Massachusetts

Dear Mr. President Roosevelt,

My Aunt Dora said I should write to you because I got a lot of questions about what's going on right now, and she says that you are the one who runs the country.

My father, Joseph Bartoletti, works in the Arnold Print Works textile mill here in North Adams, Massachusetts. He is a finishing tender. That means he puts the finished printed cloth through the drying room. They call the drying room the hot box. It is so hot that sometimes my father takes his dinner sausages and cooks them on the steam pipes. He works eighty hours a week, Mr. President Roosevelt. He works hard because there are four of us children to feed. And my Great-Aunt Ida. And my uncle and some cousins. And my Aunt Dora. She lives with us. My father is a strong man with good muscles.

Last month, the company put a sign with a big blue eagle on the front door of the mill and they had a parade and everybody clapped. Two days ago, the boss told my father that he can only work for forty hours now because of your NRA. So why are we supposed to clap and be happy with that old blue eagle sign? Last week, my father was making $20 a week and now he only gonna be making $14. He says you are president and you know best, but I'm not so sure about that. So please explain to me what you are thinking.

I have good spelling, don't you think? The reason for this is my Aunt Dora is a teacher. She made us speak English, not Italian, from the day we was born. My mother wants us to speak Italian, but my Aunt Dora says we are Americans

To learn more about the NRA and the National Industrial Recovery Act, visit winslowpress.com.

Monument Square, North Adams, Massachusetts

now, and we got to speak like Americans. She says my letter to you is good practice, so she is helping me. She says I should write more neatly. But I think you don't care how I write. If you are a good president, you will answer my questions anyway.

Your friend,

Emma Bartoletti

Emma Bartoletti

P.S. You drove through my town in July 1932 when you were trying to be president. We stood at Monument Square and yelled and waved when your car came by. I don't think you could of seen me because I was only eleven years old and much shorter then. My big brother Tony, he was fifteen, but he's pretty big. He was standing in front of me. Your car slowed down a little when it was turning from Eagle Street onto Main. Maybe you could of seen me. I was there.

October 14, 1933

The White House, Washington, D.C.

Dear Miss Emma Bartoletti,

I was very happy to get your letter, but sad to hear that your father will be taking less money home every week. I'm wondering if you have a radio, and whether you are able to listen to my fireside chats. At the end of July, I gave the country a talk on what the NRA is supposed to do and how important it is for the general prosperity of our whole country. We asked all the employers, including the owners of your father's textile mill, to establish minimum hours and wages. This means that more people can be employed, and they will have more money to buy goods. The whole country will benefit. The employers in your father's mill may not be able to raise his wages as high as they were before, but as time goes on, I believe there will be more work and more profits—for your family as well as for millions of others. So I'm asking you and many others to make sacrifices now, so that hopefully soon, we can all regain prosperity.

Do you realize that the NRA abolished child labor? This makes me happier than any other thing that's happened since I was elected president. Nobody can set you to work in a mill when you should be going to school and getting an education. The law also allows for collective bargaining. This means that your father can get together with other workers and form a union to talk to his employers. They have the right to fight for better wages and better working conditions. So, Emma, it's not all bad. Give it a chance.

I appreciate hearing from you and ask that you keep in touch and let me know more about your family and your situation. Much as Mrs. Roosevelt and I like to travel about the country, I need eyes and ears like yours to report to me from the places I cannot get to. Miss Bartoletti, you seem to

To learn more about FDR's "fireside chats" on the radio, visit winslowpress.com.

"The Spirit of the New Deal," pen-and-ink drawing by Clifford F. Berryman, July 25, 1933

me to be an honest reporter who will tell me what you and the people of North Adams are thinking about. Down here in Washington, where everybody talks and nobody listens, it is refreshing to hear a clear voice from New England.

Very sincerely yours,

Franklin D. Roosevelt

Franklin D. Roosevelt

P.S. I'm sorry I did not have a chance to meet you when I passed through North Adams in July of 1932. I often had occasion to travel through the Berkshire Hills on my way to the governor's mansion in Albany, and always found the excursion a pleasant one. Another time on the Mohawk Trail, I remember stopping at the Mountain Rose Inn for a bit of lunch. They make mighty fine hot dogs up there, and I confess to a fondness for hot dogs. You should try them.

North Adams, Massachusetts

Dear Mr. President Roosevelt,

I am glad you wrote back. My family been telling me you too busy a man to write a little Italian girl. They were wrong, and I was right.

We don't got a car, but we got a radio. My father listens to it all the time. He heard you talking about the NRA. He says for you not to pay attention to what I say. He thinks you are doing a very good job. He says that his friend Luigi got a job last week on the second shift at Arnold Print Works because my father's only working one shift. He cut your picture out of the newspaper and hung it on the wall right above our kitchen table. My mother told us not to think that you are as important as the Virgin Mary. We got a little statue of her on the wall next to the stove.

Yesterday we heard on the radio that an Italian man, Mr. Fiorello La Guardia, was elected mayor of New York City. Think of that. An Italian man as mayor of the biggest city in this country. My father says one day he will take me down to New York on a Sunday excursion trip ticket to meet him. I can't wait.

So I will tell you about my life. This is good practice for me because I want to be a writer. My mother says I will be a good writer because I got my nose in everybody's business. We got four children in the

Mayor Fiorello H. La Guardia stands to the right of his wife as he casts his ballot in the New York City mayoral election, 1933.

family. My brother Tony is sixteen, and he's a baseball pitcher. He loves Babe Ruth. He plays for the St. Anthony's Church team, but next year when he graduates from Drury High School, he's going to try out for the Sons of Italy team.

Then there's me. I was born on February 27, 1921. Now I'm twelve years old, and I'm in the sixth grade at the Haskins School. I got a younger sister, Maria Angela, who's ten, and a little brother Joey, he's eight.

We live on Witt Street. My father and his Aunt Ida, they bought the building after my father and my mother got married. It has three stories and eight apartments. The building goes down a hill, so the back door on the top floor is on Witt Street and the front door on the bottom floor is on Francis Street. We live here and so does my Aunt Ida and my Aunt Dora and my Uncle Frankie with his wife and kids, and then we rent out some apartments in the basement to Mrs. Fielding, she's an older lady and her husband is kind of sickly. We rent to the Gaionis, too. They got six kids.

But times are bad now, so when the people are in trouble, my father don't make them pay the rent. And that makes my mother mad because she says we need the money just as bad. She works at Berkshire Fine Spinning on the second shift from one to ten in the night. My mother is a little lady and she works in the spinning department. She changes the spools as they fill up. Sometimes they all fill up at once and my mother got to keep those machines running smoothly. She only got ten or fifteen minutes to eat her dinner, and she got to watch the spools at the same time. Sometimes she only got time to eat one sandwich because she's watching her spools. If the string breaks, then the machines stop and the boss yells at her. The cotton they use, sometimes it comes knotty and breaks off and she got to keep running to fix it. She walks up and down all night long. I think your NRA should say she can't work so hard because her legs get pretty tired. Last week they told her she will now make $13.20 a week because that's the NRA wage. That's better than the $12 she was making, so I am doing what you said. I am giving your NRA a chance.

My mother is making all our clothes over again for this year and I been wearing the same coat for three years. My hands and knees stick way out. I tell my mother it's time for Maria Angela to wear it, but she says then there would be no coat for me. And my Uncle Frankie really wants some work, but he can't find it. And I see them people lined up outside the church waiting for food. But my father says you can't solve all the problems at once, Mr. President. He says you know what you're doing. He says I'm an impatient person. I looked that word up in the dictionary. I think impatient ought to be spelled like this: impashunt.

I got to stop writing now because my fingers are tired. Aunt Dora is checking over this whole letter for mistakes, but I will just have to scratch them out and write over because she says I can't use any more of her school paper. Sorry if there's any mess.

I hope you like my report.

Your Italian friend,

Emma Bartoletti

Emma Bartoletti

P.S. One more thing. We walk everywhere here, but the top of the Mohawk Trail is too far for walking. That's why I never did go to that Mountain Rose Inn you talk about. I'm glad to be American, but that doesn't mean I have to eat hot dogs. They look funny to me. I think you should eat my mother's macaroni and her tomato sauce, Mr. President Roosevelt. Then you would never want to eat a hot dog again.

Emma's mother might have resembled this Italian-American woman working in a silk factory in Manchester, Connecticut.

The White House, Washington, D.C.

Dear Miss Bartoletti,

Christmas greetings to you and your family. I am enclosing a small present which I hope will encourage you to continue to write me reports on your life in North Adams. You have a keen eye for the details that bring your surroundings vividly to life, and I continue to find your opinions and impressions both informative and provocative. In any case, I would not want your Aunt Dora's job jeopardized by a scarcity in her paper supply.

Mrs. Roosevelt and I will be celebrating our first Christmas in the White House. Tomorrow the whole staff will come to my office for a party. The next day we will be entertaining the White House police force and their families. Later on, we will be giving presents to all the staff and the men who work on the grounds and to the chauffeurs and all their families. So many people work hard all year long to keep this big place running, and Mrs. R. and I want to take this opportunity to thank each of them.

Then I expect I will be reading Charles Dickens' *A Christmas Carol*, as is my usual custom, to any of my family who will sit still long enough to listen. I wonder if you have ever read this story, Emma. It is truly one of my favorites, as it says so simply how much we have to be grateful for. When I read it, I try to take on the part of each character and act it straight through. It amuses me and seems to hold the attention of my younger grandchildren. Even though they may not understand every word, they laugh at the sight of their silly old grandfather making a spectacle of himself.

Yours very sincerely,

Franklin D. Roosevelt

To learn more about North Adams, Massachusetts, visit winslowpress.com.

The Christmas tree in the East Room of the White House was especially beautiful in 1934.

North Adams, Massachusetts

Dear President Roosevelt,

Thank you for the paper and the Christmas card. I'm glad to see what the White House looks like. It seems to be a pretty big place. No wonder you have so many people working there. Maybe you can listen to the trains from your porch like I can from mine. We heard your tree-lighting speech on the radio, and my brother Tony said that you would never write to me because you thanked everybody for their cards and letters already on the radio. But he was wrong, wasn't he?

The paper is very nice, and Aunt Dora is glad that I don't have to use any more of hers. The school superintendent told our teachers that even though the local banks in town helped the city government pay their bills last year, the town

is still in trouble and there is no money for extra supplies. We have to write all our tests in pencil so we can erase them and use the paper over again. So thanks for the pencils, too.

Your Christmas letter made my Aunt Dora very happy because I had to look up six words in the dictionary. IMPRESSIONS, INFORMATIVE, PROVOCATIVE, JEOPARDIZED, OPPORTUNITY, SPECTACLE. She says I have to make a dictionary out of all those hard words you write to me. Then she says I have to use the words all over again in my letters to you. Sometimes it's not so good to have a teacher in the family. She says you are making me write better English. (But it's a lot of work, so maybe you could pick easier words next time.)

I read the newspaper to my father every night before supper. His English is getting better, too. I told my father he needs to become a citizen so he can vote for Mr. President Roosevelt next time. He says he's too busy. I tell my mother the same thing, but she's busy herself. She says women don't mess in

Aunt Dora might have looked like this Italian-American woman, c. 1938.

politics. I guess she doesn't want to make a SPECTACLE of herself. I tell her your wife, Mrs. Roosevelt, messes all the time. That's what my Aunt Dora tells me.

We live right above the train station. Every night I hear the nine o'clock whistle blowing and it's the last thing I hear before I go to sleep. I see the men hiding in the freight cars when they jump off the train. The train slows down, the doors open and they jump off, one after another, just like bugs running from something. They scatter all through town. One or two of them come up the hill to our house. My mother won't let them in. She tells them to sit on the coal box and she brings them a sandwich and a glass of water. She talks to them, but she won't let us out to listen. I don't know how they know to come here, but they always come. My brother Tony follows them down the hill when my mother isn't looking. He loves the trains. He's always hanging around by the freight yards and talking to the men.

Tony says he's going to quit school and get a real job to help the family but my father says no. Tony says he already knows everything they can teach him in school. Aunt Dora tells him he got to get that high school diploma, maybe even go to college someday when times get better. And he just walks away. He told me they got a camp of hoboes living up in the woods right near the tunnel. He says someday he going to go off and see the world like all of them. But he don't tell my mama that.

I'm sending this INFORMATIVE letter before Aunt Dora gets home so she don't see that part about Tony. I don't want to JEOPARDIZE him. Don't pay no attention to my mistakes if I did any.

Your friend,

Emma Bartoletti

Emma Bartoletti

The White House, Washington, D.C.

My dear Miss Bartoletti,

I have sympathy for your brother's love of trains. I, too, suffer from that same malady. As president I am obliged to travel a great deal. It gives me a chance to get away from Washington and see what life is like for Americans all over our great country. I take maps along with me and follow the route the train is taking. I never allow the trains to go faster than thirty-five miles an hour, which is the ideal speed for taking in the countryside as it is passing. Also, since I do not possess much strength in my legs, I find it easier to balance if the train is not racketing along at a great speed.

I am not able to hear trains from the portico in the White House and I do miss them. When I am in Hyde Park, my bedroom windows give out on the Hudson River, where the tracks run up and down along the water and I, too, often go to sleep to the wailing whistle of a train. I find it to be a close and comforting sound.

That said, I would suggest you do everything you can to keep your brother Tony from jumping a train. That is no way to see the world. It is one thing to travel as I am privileged to do and quite another to bum around from one place to another, one boxcar to the next. If your brother is unable to find work when he graduates from high school (and I am in perfect agreement with your father and Aunt Dora that he must finish, especially now that he is so close), tell him to apply to the Civilian Conservation Corps. The CCC is my pet project, one of the best things I've done since I've been in office. Young men live in camps in the forests in every state in the nation, and they do vital work.

My Uncle Theodore was the first to teach me about conserving our land and trees. Then I learned the lesson on my own. For years, I worked to make the soil on our farm in Hyde Park produce corn. I had it limed, cross-ploughed,

To learn more about the Civilian Conservation Corps, visit winslowpress.com.

A poster made by the Illinois WPA Art Project in Chicago advertises the CCC.

A YOUNG MAN'S OPPORTUNITY
CCC
FOR WORK PLAY STUDY & HEALTH
Bender
UNITED STATES
CCC
CIVILIAN CONSERVATION CORPS
APPLICATIONS TAKEN BY
ILLINOIS EMERGENCY RELIEF COMMISSION
ILLINOIS SELECTING AGENCY

and manured. Finally I figured that the poor soil had just plain run out, so I gave up and planted a forest there. I hope the trees will bring the soil back to life so that one day, if they so choose, my great-grandchildren can plant corn there again.

So, you see, I am passionate about trees. I believe the forests are the "lungs" of our land. They purify the air we breathe. They give us strength. I am determined to do everything I can to preserve them. I believe that the troubles the farmers are having in the Midwest with their dusty, parched lands comes from farming out the soil.

Nothing would give me greater pleasure than knowing that your brother Tony was out there with the other young men, planting trees, building roads, fighting to control the gypsy moth, digging fire breaks. Tell him that he will earn $30 a month, and $25 of that will be sent home to all of you. From the kind of young man you say he is, I am sure he would jump at the chance to help support his younger brothers and sisters.

Your last letter had almost no mistakes at all. I continue to make every effort to pick difficult words that will send you running to the dictionary. Please tell your Aunt Dora that I am in collusion with her!

And yes, Mrs. Roosevelt certainly does mess in politics all the time. She never gives me any peace. Her latest project is the building of fifty new houses in Arthurdale, West Virginia, where we both hope that desperately poor mining families who have no work will be able to start a new life, farming their own land. It is an ambitious project, but when something needs to be done, I have always said that my Missus is the woman to do the job!

Yours sincerely,

Franklin D. Roosevelt

To learn more about
Arthurdale, West Virginia,
visit winslowpress.com.

North Adams, Massachusetts

Dear Mr. President Roosevelt,

May 13, 1934

I see what you mean about the trees. A big, dark cloud blew up over the mountains here in the last two days. The dust was everywhere. It even got in the house when you opened the door. Maria Angela said she had a sore throat and her eyes were red, and my mother kept sweeping and sweeping, but the dust kept coming back. Some people thought it was a strange fog. Some others said there must be a huge forest fire in the mountains. One crazy old man on State Street screamed at us that the world was going to end. But you know what it was? It was dust coming from those poor farmers in the Midwest that you told me about. The papers said a strong wind picked up their dust and blew it east. We only had it for two days. We feel PRIVILEGED not to live with that dust all the time.

My Uncle Frankie doesn't have a job now. Mr. Gaioni is looking for work, too. He takes the freight off the trains and loads it on the trucks for Dibbles Lumber, but he only gets three dollars a week for that. Us Italians are proud people, Mr. President Roosevelt. We are never going to take any money if we don't work for it.

Luckily, we got a big garden along both sides of the house down the hill. My mother says we never going to starve because we got that garden. We grow everything you can think of. We got apple trees and peach trees and crabapples. We grow tomatoes and herbs and eggplant and zucchini and onions and potatoes and cucumbers and beans and lettuce. My Aunt Ida got her part of the garden and Uncle Frankie got his. We can grow everything and store it for the winter in the cellar next to the Gaioni's apartment. In the back we got a barn for tools.

We got chickens, too, and rabbits. Aunt Ida is the one who

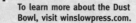

To learn more about the Dust Bowl, visit winslowpress.com.

kills the chicken for Sunday dinner. She twists the neck, and the blood spurts out and then I got to pluck it. I hate that. It smells funny and the feathers get stuck all over my fingers and I can't shake them off. She kills the rabbits and skins them, too.

Most of the people who live around us are Italian. We shop at Bushika's store down the street. He got the good Italian olive oil and macaroni for the people who don't make their own like my mother does, and tobacco for the men and cheeses and a candy counter for us kids. My mother sends me down to put something on her bill, and then Mr. Bushika slips me a piece of licorice. All the stores in town will give us Italians credit, my father says, because they know we pay our bills.

I know some people got more problems than we do, Mr. President Roosevelt. My father says we are lucky we got a house and the garden, and I know he's right.

My brother Tony graduates from Drury High School in June. He works after school and on Saturdays at the Paramount Theater. That's good because Mama can't give me money for the movies anymore. Tony lets me into the movies for free if nobody's looking. You can buy bags of popcorn for five cents, but I don't get those. For a penny, they sell you a bag of the kernels that didn't pop. They drop to the bottom. When you suck on them, they taste like real popcorn, and nobody knows you don't got real popcorn. You just got to be careful not to crack your teeth on it. But I've got real strong teeth. It must be all those good vegetables I eat. Instead of hot dogs.

I have not written to you since I got your letter because it took me all this time to look up those long words. COLLUSION? That is not fair!

Your friend,

Emma Bartoletti

Emma Bartoletti

North Adams, Massachusetts
Dear Mr. President Roosevelt,

Many things have been happening to the Bartoletti family. Last week, Tony graduated from Drury High School. The whole family went to the ceremony, and my mother couldn't stop crying because she never got past fourth grade in Italy. Think of that. And I'm already finished sixth. But my mama, she's real smart. You can get smart without going to school.

So Tony's looking for a job now. I told him about the CCC, but he says he's going to look for something that makes more money. Every day, he puts on the Sunday suit, the one my father wears to Mass, and goes out looking. He says he's going to find something because North Adams has lots of businesses. People say that's why our town is doing better than others during this Depression. Did you know we got a really famous shoe company here? It's called the Wall Streeter, and my friend Natalie's father works there. His job is to shave down the heels of the shoes so they're all level. We got quarries outside of town, and all the mills, of course, and a brickyard and railroad work. And there's lots of stores in town, like candy stores and jewelry stores and furniture stores and hat blocking stores and shoe repair stores and markets and tailors. Some of the places closed, but not too many. On the outside of town, we got farms where Tony says he might get a job bringing in the hay at the end of the summer.

Ever since my father was cut back to forty hours a week because of the *you know what*, he's been thinking and planning what he can do to bring in more money. Now he has an idea. He wants to build a greenhouse. A friend of my father's over in Williamstown been showing my father what to do. We got an old barn in the back where we keep the gardening tools and he's gonna build the greenhouse on the south side where the sun hits most of the day. My Great-Aunt Ida says my father is such a good gardener, he could make a stone grow roots. So I borrowed some books from the library and we read them at night. I have to look up really hard words for him, like humidity and seedlings and temperature. With your letters and his gardening books, I might as well just memorize the whole dictionary so I won't have to run for it all the time.

Now I got an idea, too. In the summer, I take hot supper in the middle of the day to my father at the mill. My father told me that some of the bachelor men at the mill have a lady who cooks for them up on Hall Street, but nobody to bring them the supper. So I been walking up the hill and carrying down their hot supper, and they pay me five cents each. But that's a lot of walking up and down the hill because I can't carry no more than two baskets at once. And by the time I get down the hill again, the supper isn't so hot anymore. So I'm going to get myself a bicycle. I could hang the baskets on the handlebars and strap them to the back, and that way make twenty cents or more on every trip. And I can deliver things for people around town. Emma's Delivery Service, I will call it. I looked at bicycles at Frankie's Bike Store. A new bright blue Peerless Junior costs $17.50, so I'll have to deliver a lot of suppers before I can buy that one. Frankie at the bike store says he'll let me have it if I pay a dollar a week. If I could make twenty cents every day six days a week, I could pay Frankie a dollar on Fridays and still have 20 cents left over for the movies and real popcorn. Don't you got SYMPATHY for that AMBITIOUS idea?

Your friend,

Emma Bartoletti

Emma Bartoletti

P.S. Aunt Dora read this letter and she says she's giving me a special lesson on contractions. So I'm going to get better at them. *I'm*, that's a contraction. So is *that's*, for your information. And *she's*.

August 15, 1934

The White House, Washington, D.C.

Dear Miss Bartoletti,

I have been traveling all summer down in the Caribbean, and then across our great country by train. I have just returned to Washington to find your letter. If you don't turn out to be a writer, you might well make a canny business manager. Let me know whether you ever got that Peerless Junior bicycle.

I did want to tell you that I went on a bicycle trip when I was fourteen years old. My tutor, an older fellow named

Arthur Dumper, and I traveled through Germany one summer. Arthur had an unfortunate accident with a goose who got his neck caught in the spokes of Arthur's front wheel and died. The farmer demanded we pay him for the goose, which naturally we did. That used up one full day's allowance for food and lodging so we were forced to hold to a very tight budget indeed for the rest of the trip. My advice to you is to stay out of the way of all winged animals!

I loved bicycle riding. Perhaps that's why I love to travel on trains. That sensation of being carried along on wheels makes you feel so light and easy. In Hyde Park, I have a Ford Phaeton that I drive along the back roads by means of hand controls. I also designed a special wheelchair out of a wooden kitchen chair. It is compact and fits easily into the small dumbwaiter in the back of the house. I can roll myself in and pull myself up to the second floor by means of ropes.

But I think I love sailing best of all. The wind carries you whichever way it chooses. You look down and see the water

*Franklin and Eleanor with a friend
on one of their western trips.*

To learn more about Campobello, visit winslowpress.com.

skimming by and your troubles are lifted. Anything and everything seems possible. In Washington, I can sail on the Potomac River aboard the Sequoia, but my favorite moments of all are spent on my yawl, the Amberjack II. My sons and I often sail it from Massachusetts to Campobello, our place in Canada, at the end of the summer. They are the crew, and I am the skipper. It's the last place on earth where I can order them about, and they are forced to pay attention to their old man.

One more story. This one is for your mother, who never got past the fourth grade. Somebody once said about a man: "He got a lot of book knowledge but he ain't got no nother knowledge." It is not book knowledge alone that will get you through life. You have got to have nother knowledge, too. Your mother sounds as if she's got a whole storehouse of that "nother knowledge." You can tell her that from me.

Best to you and your family,

Franklin D. Roosevelt

Franklin D. Roosevelt

P.S. Mr. James Wall of Wall Streeter Shoes is a fine, committed citizen. I know his work and have appointed him to the Massachusetts board of the NRA.

On the Amberjack II: The president is at the wheel. James is wearing a black sweater. Franklin Jr. is at the far right, and John is standing behind his father. The three people in the bow are unidentified.

September 5, 1934

North Adams, Massachusetts
Dear Mr. President Roosevelt,

I have a lot to tell you. I never did get the Peerless Junior because a friend of my father's sold me an old bicycle for only ten dollars. He let me pay him a dollar a week. It was beat-up looking, but I painted it blue. My father put a rack on the back and it only took me six weeks to pay the man back. Some days I carried five hot suppers to Arnold Print Works and four more to Wall Streeter Shoes because my friend Natalie's father told the men about my delivery service, and they signed up. So I've been busy.

But there's lots of bad news. First of all, my mama stopped working because the United Textile Workers called that big strike on all the cotton mills. Yesterday all the mills in Adams closed down. That's 2,900 people not working in this town. I heard on the radio that you told some people to find out about the problems in the textile mills and report back to you. Well, I can report to you right now that my mother used to take care of eight looms and now she has to cover twelve looms. They call that a stretch-out and the workers say it's because of that old NRA of yours. The mill owners say because the workers can only work forty hours a week, they got to do more work in those forty hours than before. That NRA was supposed to help the workers too, but everybody forgot about that part. My mother's a small woman with short legs, Mr. President Roosevelt, and when she gets home at ten o'clock from the late shift, she looks tired. My father makes her soak her feet so they won't hurt so much and keep her awake all night.

My mother goes to all the union meetings. She says she's going to start taking me because she can't understand all the things Mr. Joseph White got to say. He's the union man. And there's a woman who speaks, too.

Your reporter,

Emma Bartoletti

Emma Bartoletti

A woman separates threads in a textile mill in Taftsville, Connecticut. Background: Arnold Print Works

To learn more about the labor movement during the Depression, visit winslowpress.com.

September 12, 1934

The White House, Washington, D.C.

Dear Emma,

   I am following the textile workers' strike very closely and am deeply concerned about the increasing violence in the Southern states. I am relieved to know that the strikers in Massachusetts have remained peaceful. As you have probably read in your North Adams newspaper, last week I appointed Governor John Winant from your neighboring state of New Hampshire to head up a special board of inquiry. He will look into the complaints of the textile workers and will report to me. Please continue to send me word yourself, as I know you are on the front lines in this situation and can give me the most accurate description of conditions in the mills.

Very truly yours,

Franklin D. Roosevelt

A policeman escorts a woman mill worker after arresting her for picketing the Jackson Mill, Nashua, New Hampshire, 1934.

North Adams, Massachusetts

Dear Mr. President Roosevelt,

I don't have much time to write because I go to the union meetings with my mother most afternoons and Aunt Dora says I been skipping my homework too much. So here's my report. I got Mrs. Gaioni to give me her copy of the *North Adams Transcript* from Friday, September 7th, so I could send you this picture from the front page. My father hung the other one up on the wall between his picture of you and the statue of the Virgin Mary. I know we look like two small dots, but I circled me and my mother. We were back a ways in the crowd, so you can't really see what we look like, but that's definitely me and her because I remember the man taking the pictures.

At the union meetings, a lady named Josephine Kaczor gets up and speaks in Polish. Then a Polish lady who works in the Greylock mill says the speech over in English. Mrs. Kaczor says you can't let the foremen and the mill owners push you around anymore. She says we're people, not machines. And the crowd all jumps to their feet and cheers when they hear that. My mother jumps up and claps too. She's probably been thinking about her poor tired legs at the end of every day. She likes that a woman gets up in front of that big crowd and gives those speeches. One day she said to me maybe she's gonna learn to write her name and speak English better so she can understand.

Four thousand mill workers are on strike up here in the Northern Berkshires. But we are still trying to PRESERVE the peace. We don't go fighting with the police the way they do down South. I think you should tell that Mr. Winant and the mill owners that it's time for them to listen to the workers. We want COLLECTIVE BARGAINING. We want PROSPERITY, too. We are people, not machines. I hope you are not in

COLLUSION with the big businessmen the way people are saying you are.

People aren't saying such good things about you anymore, Mr. President Roosevelt.

Your friend,

Emma Bartoletti

Emma Bartoletti

P.S. It's a good thing the strike was called in September, because my mother has canned just about every vegetable in sight. My father says to stay out of her way or she's gonna start throwing us in the boiling water and stuffing us into quart jars. But we got a full cellar for the winter. I think we're going to need it.

Schoolchildren in Red House, West Virginia, 1935. Some children couldn't go to school because of the long hours they worked in factories.

Hyde Park, New York

Dear Emma,

Thank you for your reports on the textile workers strike. They were very helpful, as I was able to tell the members of my board of inquiry about your mother's experience with the stretch-out. Reports from the field strengthen my arguments, which is why I am always happy to hear from you. I am glad I was able to convince the unions to go back to work, but I want to assure you that we will do all we can to answer the grievances of the workers. No, I am not in COLLUSION with big businessmen. If you talk to a few of them, you'll find that they dislike me more than anybody else.

I do understand that some people are angry with me, Miss Bartoletti. This country is so large and the people have so many competing interests that it is difficult to please all of the people all of the time. I remember last spring when a steel company official said he thought it would be demeaning to sit down with William Green, the labor leader. Now, that kind of attitude from a businessman is ridiculous and does not help to solve the problems. But, on the other hand, people on the labor side can often be just as difficult.

I hope that no matter what you think of my actions, you will still write to me. I continue to value your forthright opinions and your sharp eye. We are trying to do our best, and we think we are slowly but surely improving conditions.

Very sincerely yours,

Franklin D. Roosevelt

Franklin D. Roosevelt

P.S. Perhaps your mother might like to come down to the White House and give Mrs. Nesbitt, the White House cook, some instruction. She believes that a proper diet consists of plain foods plainly prepared, but a human being can only endure so much broccoli in one lifetime. Or perhaps your Aunt Ida could teach Mrs. Nesbitt the secret of rabbit stew. I love the taste of fresh game.

Mrs. Henry Nesbitt

October 2, 1934

North Adams, Massachusetts

Dear Mr. President Roosevelt,

I know you're trying to fix things in the country, and I don't believe you're forgetting us poor people. But we got our GRIEVANCES. The mills in Adams didn't get running again for another week, so my mother just started her shift yesterday. She is glad the strike is over, and she thinks you were right to tell everybody to go back to work. But Mr. White, the union man, and a lot of the workers don't think the owners and the foremen will make things better in the mills, so you'd better watch them. They are rich, sneaky people who make promises they don't keep. I tell everybody that you are a CANNY president who keeps his promises. I hope I'm right.

I got more bad news. Tony left. He never did find a job this summer and it made him real mad because nobody had nothing for him. He even went down to the CCC office like you said, but they told him they couldn't take him because he was only seventeen and his family wasn't on no relief. Now, that seems stupid to me, Mr. President Roosevelt. Seems to me you should help the people who have tried like us not to take no money from the government. Then they called this strike, and Tony felt real bad because we didn't have as much money and nobody would give him a job. So one day we come home and his note was sitting there on the kitchen table under a loaf of Mama's bread. It said a big strong man like him wasn't going to take no more food from out of the mouths of me and Maria Angela and little Joey. He said he was sure he could find work out west, and he'd send money real soon. He must of wanted to go pretty bad if he left the Sons of Italy team. Lucky it's almost the end

50

To learn more about
Charles Lindbergh, visit
winslowpress.com.

of the season. I know Tony's going to be mad that Babe Ruth quit the Yankees. I wish he had hit a home run in that last game with them. My father and me, we are keeping all the stats for Tony for when he gets home.

Mr. Lindbergh was such a brave man to fly across the ocean all by himself so I'm glad they caught the man who stole his baby. What a horrible thing that kidnapper did. It's good that Maria Angela and Joey sleep in the same room with me, because I won't let nobody come and kidnap them in the middle of the night.

I wish Tony would come home.
I miss him.

Your friend,

Emma Bartoletti
Emma Bartoletti

Charles Lindbergh

The White House, Washington, D.C.

Dear Emma,

I was so sorry to hear that Tony left for out West. From all you've told me about him, he seems an honest and intelligent young man. I hope that very soon he will turn around and come home. Please let me know when you hear from him.

Today is Mrs. Roosevelt's fiftieth birthday, but she will be celebrating it in New York, where she is campaigning for Caroline O'Day, who is running for Congress. She always takes a great interest in the doings of the Bartoletti family. I know she will be joining me in prayers for Tony's safe return when I tell her what has happened.

Very truly yours,

Franklin D. Roosevelt

Caroline O'Day was Congressional representative-at-large from New York State for four terms, 1934-42.

To learn more about Caroline O'Day, visit winslowpress.com.

Eleanor Roosevelt, 1932

November 8, 1934

North Adams, Massachusetts

Dear Mr. President Roosevelt,

This is to let you know that we heard two times from Tony. It was just postcards, and this is what he said. I have copied it right from the cards. Mama has them stuck up on the wall next to the Virgin Mary. We pray to her every night to bring him home soon.

The first card came from Dubuque, Iowa in October. I went to the library and brought home an atlas so we could look at the town on a map. Mama cried when she saw how far away it was from us. He's almost halfway across the country.

> Dear Family,
> I'm okay. Don't worry. I've got friends and I am seeing a lot of places. Nobody's got jobs but I'm getting along. Emma, go look for a sign of a cat near the back porch. That's how come all the men knock at our house for food. Your boy, Tony

He was right. There was a chalk picture of a cat on the side of the coal box. Now, when the men come, Mama asks if they've seen Tony. They say no, but they say he'll be okay. The boys on the road look out for each other. Aunt Ida says Mama gives them too much to eat, but Mama keeps thinking it means some woman out there in Iowa will be feeding Tony.

The second card came from Omaha, Nebraska, so he didn't get so much farther. We just pray he'll turn around soon and come back home.

> Dear Family,
> I'm getting along. I can't send you any money yet, but I'm okay. Emma, you write that president and tell him people are starving out here in the country. I've seen whole families on the road looking for work. You stay in North Adams. Things are better there than anywhere I've seen. Tony

So I'm telling you the way he asked me to. Maybe he'll come home now. We say a novena for him every week. Mama keeps her rosary beads in her pocket, and her lips are always praying.

Mama says she's still got the twelve looms, so they kept up the stretch-out. She thinks you ought to know that.

The Democrats won almost all the elections here. You should watch out for Vermont. It looks like the whole state voted Republican, except in Readsboro where all the Italians live. I know because I've been reading the newspaper to my father.

Your friend,

Emma Bartoletti

Emma Bartoletti

P.S. Please tell Mrs. Roosevelt that I hope she had a nice birthday.

Two boys hitch a ride on a train to upper New York State

December 21, 1934

The White House, Washington, D.C.

Dear Emma,

Mrs. Roosevelt and I send Christmas greetings to you and your family with wishes for a happy and prosperous New Year. You have used up a great deal of paper in writing me your reports, so I am sending a package of replacements as well as more pencils. Yours must be worn down to nothing by now. Also, Mrs. R. asked me to send along this vest. She is never without her knitting needles. She is not sure whether this will fit you or your sister Maria Angela, but she is hoping it will keep one of you warm through the winter ahead.

This year we shall hold the tree lighting ceremony in Lafayette Park since so many people now attend. They say they are expecting a crowd of 10,000. They have planted one of the Fraser firs directly west of the monument of Andrew Jackson. This gives me great pleasure, because I consider him to have been a courageous and patriotic citizen.

I was glad to have your warning about the state of Vermont.

Yours very sincerely,

Franklin D. Roosevelt

February 14, 1935

North Adams, Massachusetts

Dear Mr. President Roosevelt,

We were all happy to get that picture of you and Mrs. President Roosevelt, too. We have put the Christmas card you sent up on the wall above the kitchen table. The vest fit Maria Angela just right, and she is telling everybody she meets that Eleanor Roosevelt knitted it for her. Some people don't believe her, but I tell her not to pay any attention to them.

Thank you for the pencils and the paper. I think I have enough now to write a book, but my mother says I will use it up very quickly because I always got so much to say. Here is some of my mother's tomato sauce. She's worried the glass jar will break in the mail, but I packed lots of newspapers around it.

I also heard on the radio the other day that you collect stamps so Aunt Ida said I could take the stamp from her letter from Italy and send it to you. She still has family near Lake Garda, and they write to her. I hope you don't have one of these already. I don't want this to be a REPLACEMENT. Let me know if there's anything else you collect. Maybe I can help you along with your other collections.

Your friend,

Emma Bartoletti

Emma Bartoletti

Eleanor Roosevelt's hands were seldom idle. Here she is knitting at a table at Hyde Park.

March 1, 1935

The White House, Washington, D.C.

Dear Emma,

Your mother's tomato sauce is exquisite (run to the dictionary). You can assure her the glass jar did not break, and the taste on my tongue reminded me of summer. Mrs. Nesbitt had a bit herself and said it was quite good. Thank you also for the stamp, which is a new one in my collection and not a REPLACEMENT at all. Not even a duplicate. I am often up late at night working on my stamp collection and find the pastime soothing after a hectic day running the country!

I am a confirmed collector of all sorts of things. When I was growing up in Hyde Park, I was fascinated by the different species of birds. I was given a small-calibre rifle and my father allowed me to shoot one pair of birds from each species found in the Hudson River valley. But there were other rules and requirements. I was not allowed to shoot a nesting pair or any bird at all during the mating season, and I had to learn to stuff and mount the birds myself. This last part I found very unpleasant, and once I had mastered the skill, I was able to convince my parents to allow a professional to take over the job. I am quite proud of my collection, which is kept in a glass cabinet in the front hall of Springwood, our Hyde Park house. It numbers over three hundred specimens in all.

As I told you, I love sailing, and have been interested in

Inset: FDR as assistant secretary of the Navy
Background: FDR, who owned more than a million stamps,
gazes at his stamp collection through a magnifying glass.

To learn more about Hyde Park, visit winslowpress.com.

ships of all kinds for most of my life. For some time I was the assistant secretary of the Navy, and this gave me a great opportunity to expand my knowledge. I have managed to collect hundreds of books and paintings as well as ship models and log books and other miscellany. Mrs. Roosevelt wonders sometimes how we shall ever find room for all of these things. She is mighty happy that none of our children have become collectors.

I wonder if you are a collector of anything.

Have you heard anything more from Tony?

Very sincerely,

Franklin D. Roosevelt

Inset: President Roosevelt examining a toy sailboat while son John watches from the background on Roosevelt's private yacht in Campobello Island, Canada.

March 27, 1935

North Adams, Massachusetts
Dear Mr. President Roosevelt,

I am not a collector of anything because I don't like to stay in one place for too long. I guess collecting stamps is good for you. I know that your legs are not strong

because of your malady, the infantile paralysis. I didn't have to look any of those words up in the dictionary because I read them in the paper all the time. We had an epidemic here when I was little and since then, my mother won't let us go swimming at the Fish Pond in the summer. The other mothers say the same thing. I don't mean to be rude to mention your affliction. My father finally built the greenhouse off the side of the barn, and my Uncle Frankie and Mr. Gaioni, they all helped. They made a cement foundation, and then they put in the support beams and the glass which we got from a man over in Williamstown. (I know all these words because my father and I been reading for one whole year about greenhouses.) He put in a wheel to turn open the

FDR enjoys a relaxed moment at Hyde Park.

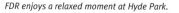

To learn more about FDR's health and infantile paralysis, visit winslowpress.com.

windows. Then he built wooden benches and planted all the seeds. As soon as the plants are up, I'm going to put them in my bicycle basket and take them around to sell in the neighborhood. We're selling tomatoes and basil and pepper plants. And other vegetables and flowers, too. It is an EXQUISITE greenhouse.

We are all working hard to make sure we have some extra money, because that old NRA of yours looks like it's going to shut the mills down again. We read something in the paper about it yesterday. Working so hard makes us not think all the time about Tony who does not write anymore. I told Mama maybe he doesn't have enough money for stamps. Not even one cent for a postcard, she says, and that makes her look sick. So I wish I had shut my mouth.

Your friend,

Emma Bartoletti

Emma Bartoletti

P.S. The Children of Mary Society at my church did a play called "La Croce di Marmo" (The Cross of Marble) for Lent. I played Mary Magdalene. I like riding my bike better.

April 10, 1935

The White House, Washington, D.C.

Dear Emma,

I was very impressed with the word "affliction." I almost had to run for the dictionary myself. I do not think you are rude at all. I travel often to Warm Springs, Georgia, and find  my legs grow stronger because of the warm-water therapy there. (It is 88 degrees.) I've started a foundation, which I hope one day soon will find a cure for infantile paralysis. It would be nice if you could swim in the Fish Pond without your mother worrying.

Your father sounds like a most enterprising man. I, too, have a greenhouse in Hyde Park, and it does me good to see the green shoots poking out of the soil as early as March and to know that the growing season is around the corner.

I wish you continued success in your delivery business.

Very sincerely yours,

Franklin D. Roosevelt

Franklin D. Roosevelt

P.S. I sympathize with your loving your bike better than acting in a play. I recently went to the dentist, and most days, I like being president better than having my teeth drilled.

North Adams, Massachusetts

Dear Mr. President Roosevelt,

Just like I said, my mother is out of work again because the Berkshire Spinning Works is shut down for the week and maybe longer. Three thousand people <u>can't</u> work because the bosses say that too much cotton was being made and not enough people were buying it and the NRA <u>wouldn't</u> let them make any more. Someone wrote in the paper that nobody was buying because the NRA prices were too high. I <u>don't</u> know who's right. Arnold Print Works <u>isn't</u> shut down. They print the patterns on the cotton, so they <u>don't</u> get shut down as quickly. And my Aunt Dora still has her teaching job. Uncle Frankie got himself a job building roads, so he can pay a little rent this month. And <u>I've</u> started my bike delivery service again. Mr. Bushika is giving me work, and the seedling plants will be ready to deliver soon if we still get the good weather. So the Bartolettis are okay. My mother says to tell you that the NRA <u>doesn't</u> listen to the workers but I tell her <u>you're</u> trying lots of different things, and some of them are working even if others <u>aren't</u>.

For your information, <u>it's</u> always better when my mother is working. She worries so much when she stays at home that she runs us all around in circles. Me especially, because <u>I'm</u> the oldest girl and the oldest one at home. My father says if she weeds the garden one more time, there <u>won't</u> be a plant left in it. And when <u>she's</u> at work, <u>I'm</u> the one in charge of the house after school. Me and Joey and Maria Angela listen to the Green Hornet and the Lone Ranger on the radio. But when she stays home, she <u>won't</u> let us do that.

Maybe Tony will come home soon, and Mama can fuss over him instead of the rest of us. I lie in bed at night and hear the trains coming through the Hoosac Tunnel. I think

To learn more about popular radio shows, visit winslowpress.com.

The western entrance of the Hoosac Tunnel, North Adams, Massachusetts

somewhere out there my brother <u>Tony's</u> riding one of them trains. I keep praying that the door will open and <u>he'll</u> be here home with us again.

I put a line under every one of my contractions because Aunt Dora said I should use all the ones I can. I used a lot, <u>didn't</u> I?

Your friend,

Emma Bartoletti

Emma Bartoletti

P.S. <u>I'm</u> IMPRESSED that Babe Ruth hit a home run at opening day, but it feels funny to be rooting for a Boston team even though <u>it's</u> in Massachusetts. I like the Yankees better. I heard you threw out the first ball for the Senators yesterday. It's UNFORTUNATE you <u>couldn't</u> throw out a DUPLICATE one for the Yankees.

The White House, Washington, D.C.

Dear Emma,

I'm sorry to hear that your mother is out of work again, especially since it interrupts your afternoon radio shows! I still believe that the NRA has done much to improve working conditions in this country, even though it means the factories have to be shut down from time to time. But I certainly hope that with your father's work and your expanding delivery service, the Bartoletti family will get through yet another rough patch. If only Tony would come home!

I've just signed an executive order to create something called the Works Progress Administration (WPA), because we still need to get more people back to work. I want the projects to be useful, and I want them to get the greatest number of people off the relief rolls. As usual, Mrs. Roosevelt has been doing her part. She has been organizing what work women should do in the WPA. She and her committee have decided that the projects should include jobs such as book repair in libraries and the creation of guidebooks to each of the states, as well as the keeping of historical records and the writing of new plays. Once she has her mind set on something, there's no stopping Mrs. R. I have a feeling that's true of Miss Emma Bartoletti, too.

Yours sincerely,

Franklin D. Roosevelt

Eleanor Roosevelt, 1933

To learn more about the Works Progress Administration, visit winslowpress.com.

June 4, 1935

North Adams, Massachusetts
Dear Mr. President Roosevelt,

My Aunt Dora says that it is not polite to say "I told you so," but I heard that your NRA was knocked down by the Supreme Court. You have my SYMPATHY because I know you think it was really helping the country, but it wasn't much helping the Bartoletti family in North Adams, Massachusetts. My mother still isn't back to working. She's been out since the end of April. Some of the union leaders are talking about striking again, but my mother doesn't think that's a good idea because it didn't do her any good last time. Do you know what some people called the NRA? They called it the National Runaround, because you promised to help the everyday people and then nothing ever come of it for the workers. I tell people you are our friend and that you are a very busy man trying to take care of so many problems at once, but they are still grumbling.

But I have better news than that. Tony came home. Our prayers worked! One day when I was piling plants into my bike basket, I looked down the hill and I seen this man walking up the back way from the train depot. I thought, it's one of those hoboes coming up for food. And it was. Except it was Tony. I screamed for my mother and dropped my bike. I ran down that hill and hugged him so hard, he almost fell over. The whole street came out and yelled hello. He was dirty and smelled like smoke and the railroad and sweat, and he was wearing some worn-out pants with a rope run through to hold them up and a beat-up old cap. He's been home a week now, but he still looks real tired.

To learn more about hoboes, visit winslowpress.com.

He looks like an old man. He made it all the way to Denver, Colorado, before he turned around and headed home. I showed him the map of the country I had to draw for geography class. He drew a line to all the places he went. He's seen a whole lot of this United States.

Tony says one day he's going to tell me what he saw out there in the country so I can write you about it.

Your friend,

Emma Bartoletti

Emma Bartoletti

P.S. Tony can't believe that Babe Ruth quit baseball. But we don't blame him. Those Boston Braves weren't treating him right. Even after he hit those three home runs out of Forbes field in Pittsburgh. Nobody ever did that before.

Tony might have resembled this young farm worker, 1935.
Background: A hobo sits by the railroad tracks.

June 16, 1935

The White House, Washington, D.C.

Dear Emma,

Mrs. Roosevelt and I were overjoyed to learn that Tony had returned home safely. I would like to hear what he has to say about his travels. In May, Mrs. R took a trip to the bottom of a coal mine shaft in the state of Ohio. She was able to see four hundred miners at work. The conditions in those mines are pretty rough, and from what I hear, she looked mighty dirty herself when she came back up. She said she couldn't imagine being out on the road the way Tony traveled with no place to take a bath and no way of knowing where his next meal was coming from. We both hope your mother's good cooking has restored Tony to his old self.

I know you never thought the NRA did your family any good, and now it appears that for different reasons, the Supreme Court has agreed with Miss Emma Bartoletti of North Adams, Massachusetts. I hope they don't choose to dismantle the rest of our legislation. It seems to me that it is common sense to take a method and try it. If it fails, admit it frankly and try another, but, above all, try something. The NRA was created with all the best intentions, but it fell short of its goals. I'm sure you've read that prominent labor leaders such as Mr. Green of the Labor Advisory Board to the NRA and your Mr. Gorman of the Textile Workers Union have also denounced the Supreme Court decision. Nobody wants a return to child labor and a time when there were no minimum hours and wages. I just hope Mr. Gorman and the other labor officials don't call a strike as that will only makes matters worse. Who knows when your mother will ever be able to go back to work if that should happen.

I, too, shall miss Babe Ruth. I'm the kind of baseball fan who likes to get plenty of action for his money... the biggest kick out of the biggest score. The Bambino always delivered.

Very sincerely yours,

Franklin D. Roosevelt

Franklin D. Roosevelt

A miner and mule at the American Radiator Company mine,
Mt. Pleasant, Pennsylvania, c. 1936

To learn more about the case against the NRA, visit winslowpress.com.

North Adams, Massachusetts
Dear Mr. President Roosevelt,

They started the mills back up again. They called in the spinners last Wednesday, so my mother's been working for four days.

Tony got a job a few hours a day unloading the lumber from the freight cars. Mr. Gaioni talked to some of the people over at Dibbles Lumber and they took him on. But he only makes $3 a week. My mother doesn't like him going down to those railroad yards again.

He told me a little about his traveling life. Not too much, because he says the stories aren't pretty, and that I'm too

young to hear them. The men on the trains were roaming around looking for work. There was none anywhere. Some times he saw whole families traveling on the trains. Little kids like Joey and Maria Angela. Some towns wouldn't even let the strangers in. They had signs that told strangers to go away. There were bulls (that's what he calls police) waiting for the trains when they came into the stations. They shined a flashlight in your face and waved a gun at you and marched you up to the jail and DENOUNCED you. Tony said that happened to him twice, but he almost didn't mind because he was so hungry. At least he could sleep on a cot and eat something. But one

Workers in the Thread, Inc. Mill at Gastonia, North Carolina, put away spools after demonstrators persuade them to close down the mill.

night in a jail, a man stole the Miraculous Medal right off his neck when he was sleeping. My mother gave him that medal on his first communion and he wore it around his neck his whole life. It has a picture of the Virgin Mary and a prayer just to her. After that happened, Tony turned around and started trying to get home because he knew he wouldn't be safe no more.

He didn't like the West like he thought he would. He missed all the green. Now he looks up at the hills and he says to me, "Emma, all those trees have enough water. Isn't that something?" I think his time on the road made him a little crazy in the head.

Mama worries he's going to get back on a train. But I don't think he's got any INTENTIONS like that. I don't think he ever wants to be so hungry again.

The Sons of Italy team took him back, but he's got to practice a lot because his arm got weak from being on the road. Lifting the lumber is building him up again. And Mama's macaroni. That's building him up more than anything. Better than hot dogs. I bet Mama's spaghetti suppers would build your legs up, too. You tell Mrs. Nesbitt that from me.

Your friend,

Emma Bartoletti

Emma Bartoletti

Background: A textile mill in Lowell, Massachusetts, where employees worked all night.

July 22, 1935

The White House, Washington, D.C.

Dear Emma,

Thank you for passing along Tony's impressions. I understand what he means about the West. When I saw the vast emptiness of the Grand Canyon, I remember thinking how dead it looked. It made me homesick for my home in the Hudson Valley, where the trees are vital and alive. I would urge him once again to apply to the CCC. From what you wrote me, he has a new appreciation for the Berkshire hills and forests. He could become a part of preserving them and help support all of you at the same time. The work will certainly build him up again.

I have no doubt that a regular diet of your mother's cooking would have a wondrous effect on me. Mrs. Nesbitt has been feeding me oatmeal every morning at breakfast and brussel sprouts at lunch. If I eat one more bowl of oatmeal, my brains will turn to mush. However, I must report to you that she is as enthusiastic about hot dogs as I am, and for this I am grateful.

Very sincerely yours,

Franklin D. Roosevelt

The Grand Canyon, Arizona

North Adams, Massachusetts

Dear Mr. President Roosevelt,

Tony left for Fort Devens about ten days ago. He enlisted in the 1171st Company of the CCC. They let him in because now he's eighteen years old, and they're finally taking people who aren't on the dole.

His company came through here from Fort Devens last Friday on a special car at the back of the regular Boston and Maine train. I watched them load into trucks at the depot. He waved at me. He looked handsome in his uniform. He's going to be up at the Savoy Camp. Pray that this winter isn't too cold. Last year, they had to move everybody out of that camp because the weather got bad and the men almost froze to death. But they rebuilt the camp, and Tony said they got 400 cords of wood from thinning the forests last year. So that should keep them warm this winter. He gets to come down to town on Saturday nights to the movies. And soon, he'll be giving us $25 a month. The boys whose families are on the dole, the government sends the check right to the families. But not Tony. He gets paid directly and he brings us the money himself. He's real excited about that.

I start eighth grade next week. I'm going to make a Haskins School newspaper. My teacher from last year said I could do it and Aunt Dora says she'll help me when she has time.

That Social Security Act is a good thing. Now, at last the old people will have something to live on. And the Wagner Act you signed. Maybe the businessmen will have to talk to the unions now and do some COLLECTIVE BARGAINING. I'm telling everybody that you never did forget us workers, even though you are a PROMINENT person.

Your friend,

Emma Bartoletti

Emma Bartoletti

To learn more about the Social Security Act and the Wagner Labor Relations Act, visit winslowpress.com.

Inset: CCC workers in Beltsville, Maryland, 1935. Background: CCC workers wash up in Camp Rock Creek, California.

September 15, 1935

Hyde Park, New York

Dear Emma,

I was delighted to learn that you were pleased with the Social Security Act and the Wagner Labor Relations Act. As I told my cabinet the other day, if I can please my Missus and my twelve-year-old friend, Emma, then I must be doing something right. They are my two toughest critics.

Mrs. Roosevelt has come up with another brilliant idea, and it's one I think you'll like, too. She's been worried for a long time that we're going to lose this generation of young people. There are so many like Tony who are still out there riding the trains or are discouraged and out of work and unskilled. We're setting up something called the National Youth Administration (NYA) to give grants to high school and college students in return for work. That way, we hope they will stay in school as long as possible. The tougher task will be to train kids like Tony who have graduated from school but can't find any work. But we're going to try. I hope Tony will approve of this plan. Please continue to send me news of him. Decades from now, his grandchildren will walk under the trees he is planting this year. Just think of that!

Very sincerely yours,

Franklin D. Roosevelt

To learn more about the National Youth Administration, visit winslowpress.com.

A poster from the Illinois branch of the NYA promoting educational opportunities for young men seeking training for employment

ILLINOIS
NATIONAL YOUTH ADMINISTRATION

BOYS – ARE YOU
INTERESTED IN A JOB?

FIND OUT WHAT AN OCCUPATION HAS TO OFFER YOU IN
PAY-EMPLOYMENT-SECURITY AND PROMOTION

FREE CLASSES
IN OCCUPATIONS

ON   AT

THE SUBJECT WILL BE

WM. J. CAMPBELL, STATE DIRECTOR

October 21, 1935

North Adams, Massachusetts
Dear Mr. President Roosevelt,

First of all, I am not twelve years old anymore. I am fourteen and a half!

Here's what Tony does every day. He gets up at 6 A.M., washes up, and then eats breakfast at big, long tables. Most of the other boys come from cities in the East and the Midwest. He bunks next to a boy from Dubuque, Iowa, one of the places he went to on the train. Some of the other boys had been riding the rails, too, and they looked even punier than him when they first came. They came right off the trains and didn't have Mama's food to build them up. But now they're all getting thick muscles. They work from eight to lunchtime, come back to the camp for food, and then work all afternoon. They already got a baseball team, and Tony's pitching, so he's keeping his arm in shape. They have classes most days, and Tony's learning about making photographs. Some of the kids never finished high school, so they're taking classes to graduate. Saturdays they come down to town and Tony always stops in to see us and sometimes brings a friend or two. He says to tell you that he

CCC workers construct an irrigation canal

thinks that Mrs. Roosevelt's NYA idea is a good one. If he could have gotten a job last summer, he doesn't think he would have jumped on that train.

Tony says they got lots of projects going on up at Savoy Camp. First they been rebuilding the Black Brook Road where it connects to the Mohawk Trail. They want to finish before the snow comes so they can get in and out. I told Tony if he ever wants a hot dog, he should go to that Mountain Rose Inn you wrote me about. Then, this winter they got 150 acres of forest to clean up and thin out so the big trees can grow. In the spring, they'll be planting trees.

I started the school paper. It's hard writing that much, but a boy named Felix is helping me and my friend Natalie, too. When I get out of school in the middle of the day, I'm still taking four suppers to the men in the mills. I'm going to keep riding my bike till it snows.

Last week a boy Joey's age died in the next town of that infantile paralysis. They made all the kids in his brother's and sister's grades go home and stay out of school. They won't let any children in that town go to the movies. Nobody in North Adams got it this year. So far.

Your friend,

Emma Bartoletti

Emma Bartoletti

 To learn more about the Mohawk Trail, visit winslowpress.com.

83

December 22, 1935

The White House, Washington, D.C.

Dear Emma,

Christmas greetings to you and your family. This is a photograph of Mrs. Roosevelt and myself in front of the Executive Office. I am sending along my customary present. It seems to me that between the school newspaper you are publishing and your letters to me, you must once again be running short of paper and pencils. Please see the enclosed.

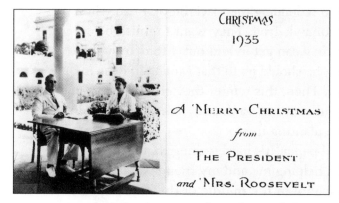

I have a bad headache and am going to turn in early. Mrs. R. says I have been doing too much. Running this great big country of ours can tire a person out from time to time.

Yours very sincerely,

Franklin D. Roosevelt

Franklin D. Roosevelt

P.S. Please accept my apologies for misstating your age. As my secretary and the members of the Congress will tell you, I often get my numbers muddled.

Above: The black-and-white image on the Roosevelts' 3¹/₂ x 5¹/₂-inch Christmas card in 1935. President and Mrs. Roosevelt are seated at a drop-leaf table in front of the Executive Office. At right: Exterior view of the White House at Christmas, showing lit evergreen trees

January 20, 1936

North Adams, Massachusetts
Dear Mr. President Roosevelt,

I am writing to you in the middle of a blizzard. We hope
Tony and his camp have enough wood to get through this
one. Thank you for the paper. It's very nice you sent it to
me, especially this year. I told my parents that I am giving
them a good Christmas present. I am teaching them to
read and write English. Then they can pass that test and
be citizens, so they are using the paper and the pencils,
too. I teach my mother in the morning at breakfast and on
Saturday afternoons. I teach my father at night after dinner.
I won't let him listen to the radio till he's done his lessons.
Now I make him read the newspaper to me. He says I make
them work very hard, but they have a lot to learn. They've
got to answer all these questions about American history
and how the government works. I bet there are some
American-born citizens who can't answer those questions.
Why the thirteen stripes in the flag? What is a republic?
What happens if a President vetoes a bill? They've got to
swear not to be an anarchist or a polygamist. My mother
thought that was a pretty funny question. She says one
husband is enough for her. Then they've got to memorize
the Pledge of Allegiance. I know it by heart because we say
it every day in school.

My father tried to read me something in the paper today
about the NRA, but it was hard, so I took the paper back
and read to him. It says that your BOARD OF INQUIRY
found out that the mill owners are making everybody work
longer hours again since the NRA ended. And those owners
are not paying overtime. Didn't I tell you they were sneaky

people? My mother and father are working the same hours as before, but my mother still got the twelve looms she's got to watch. And my friend Natalie, her father is working longer hours over at Wall Streeter Shoes again. And he's not paid any extra. You should write your friend Mr. Wall about that.

SINCERELY, your friend,

Emma Bartoletti

Emma Bartoletti

February 21, 1936

The White House, Washington, D.C.

Dear Emma,

I think you will be pleased to hear that I have just appointed Matthew T. Abbruzzo to be one of fifteen federal judges in the Eastern District of New York. After confirmation by the full Senate on February 12, he was sworn into office today. I do believe he is the first federal judge of Italian origin ever chosen, and I wanted you to know that your example has taught me a great deal about the spirit and intelligence of the Italian people. I hope that one day you will go to New York and see for yourself what Mayor La Guardia is doing there. Even though he and I are on opposite sides of the political fence, we agree wholeheartedly on the need to help the forgotten people who have nobody else to fight for them.

Is it possible, Miss Emma Bartoletti, that you are admitting in a sideways manner that the bad old NRA might have been good for something? At least it made those mill owners behave themselves for a while.

Sincerely yours,

Franklin D. Roosevelt

Franklin D. Roosevelt

President Roosevelt chatting with Mayor Fiorello H. La Guardia

North Adams, Massachusetts

Dear Mr. President Roosevelt,

We've been having a bad time up here in North Adams. This time it is not the mill owners or the government or the good old NRA. It's the weather. All month the rivers have been flooding. They closed the schools, they closed Arnold Print Works, and one night my mother couldn't get home from work in Adams because State Street was washed out. She and my Aunt Dora slept in the school on the classroom floor. Natalie's family lives on State Street and they had to leave their house because the water started to come in the front door. They grabbed their clothes and ran up the hill to us. They lived with us for four days and when they got back home, their furniture was soaked through and their chickens had been washed down the river. Natalie's father went to work extra time because the Wall Streeter factory got flooded, and Mr. Wall asked everybody to haul the shoes out so they could dry in the sun. Natalie and I went by after school to help. There was a huge pile of shoes and wooden lasts and rubber heels tumbled on top of each other in the yard. Mr. Wall gave everybody a party when the work was done, but I heard some of the men saying, we want wages for the job we done. We don't need no party.

If I have time, I'm going to make a special flood edition of the *Haskins Herald*. That's the name for my newspaper.

Last month before the rains, Tony and another guy saw two children stealing scraps from the Savoy camp garbage heap. The kids looked pitiful. They had skin sores, and they were dressed in burlap sacks and had nothing but rags for shoes. Tony got the little boy to lead him back to the rest of his family, who were living in some old, rundown shack. He said the place smelled something terrible, and one of the

March 22, 1936

90

other children had a frozen ear. All of them huddled in one single bed trying to keep warm. Even the mother and the father. The water on the floor of the cabin was frozen solid. Tony told Mr. Churchill, his camp commander, and the family was taken down into the town of Florida by a state patrolman. I hope the town gave them some food and shelter. It would be scary to spend the winter up in that forest if you didn't have any food or any way to keep yourself warm. Tony said he'd seen people starving like that when he was riding on the trains, but he was ADMITTING he didn't ever think it could happen near here. I guess bad things can happen anywhere.

I got to go now. Mama says it's time to go to Mass, and we've got plenty of people to pray for. Then, when we get home, she has to write out one whole page in English. She's only got two months before the citizenship test. If I don't turn out to be a writer or a businessman, then maybe I'll be a teacher like my Aunt Dora.

Your friend,

Emma Bartoletti

Emma Bartoletti

Inset: Shoes drying in the sun after the flood.
Background: A view of North Adams from one of the houses on Witt Street

May 4, 1936

The White House, Washington, D.C.

Dear Emma,

Thank you for the report on the floods in North Adams. Flooding was widespread in many of the New England states this spring, and especially in the Connecticut Valley. The government is working with all the affected states to put together a flood control plan. I hope one day a rising river will not cause your friend Natalie to flee her house.

I wish you had been here last night. Mrs. Roosevelt invited fifteen members of the National Women's Trade Union League to stay this week at the White House during their convention. She was not here when they arrived, and so I welcomed them. A number of us had a rousing talk about labor conditions in the country. Among others, the group included a waitress, a stenographer, a garment worker from New York, and a textile worker from Alabama. I thought of your mother. I bet she would have had lots to say in this group. They told me that since the NRA was dismantled by the Supreme Court, wages have been lowered, work hours have been lengthened and children are being hired again to work in the mills. This disheartened me. As one of them said, we simply can't look to the captains of industry to solve the problems of the employed. I told them that all of us must continue to fight for the rights of the working people in this country. I left them talking away in the sitting room when I went up to bed.

And yes, Emma, sad to say, bad things can happen anywhere.

Your friend,

Franklin D. Roosevelt

Franklin D. Roosevelt

To learn more the National Women's Trade Union League, visit winslowpress.com.

Three boys walking home from work in Ambridge, Pennsylvania, 1938

June 30, 1936

North Adams, Massachusetts
Dear Mr. President Roosevelt,

Seems like good things happen to the Bartoletti family and then bad things right after that.

Here's the good thing. My parents are now American citizens. They both passed their tests. The court opened at 9 A.M. and I skipped school so I could go with them. Then a man examined them. I couldn't go in the room, but they must have done all right because he read off their names to be citizens. I was so excited. My mother told me later she was the only one in the room who knew how many members we elect to the State Legislature from our county. Not even my father could remember that. My mother is really smart with numbers. She could probably help you out when you get MUDDLED.

Soon they're going to register to vote, and I told them they better vote for you if they know what's good for them. But they don't need me telling them that. My mother says, I didn't get through school, but I can vote. Think of that. She started to cry after she said that. We had a big party, and all the neighbors came. Aunt Ida cooked two chickens and a rabbit to celebrate. When they get their papers from the clerk of the Superior Court, we are going to frame them and hang them on the kitchen wall next to the Christmas card of you and Mrs. Roosevelt. Then there will be no more room on that wall at all.

They know you got nominated for president again. I read them part of your acceptance speech out of the newspaper. It was awful long, but my mother liked the part you said about the citizen's right to work and then the other part about industrial dictatorship.

These four images of FDR show his congenial nature.

Now here's the bad news. My Aunt Dora's been fired. She was the best teacher in the school. Everybody loved her. The school principal told her the budget was cut, and he didn't have a choice. But nobody else in the school got fired. She thinks she got fired because she was the only Italian teacher and she still speaks with an accent. Also, she is a single woman and doesn't have children to support. The school superintendent came by to see her. His little girl was in her class last year, and he said he was very sorry, but he couldn't change what the principal decided to do.

She was making $20 a week. So now that money is gone. Lucky my father planted extra in the greenhouse. It looks like I'm going to be delivering even more plants. At least we've still got the money coming in from Tony.

Your friend,

Emma Bartoletti

Emma Bartoletti

 To learn more about FDR's four inaugural addresses, visit winslowpress.com.

The White House, Washington, D.C.

Dear Emma,

My heartiest congratulations to your parents on their citizenship. Hardworking, involved people like Mr. and Mrs. Joseph Bartoletti are exactly what this country needs to move forward into a future filled with promise.

Now, as to your Aunt Dora, I have an idea for her. Remember I wrote you about the Works Progress Administration, the new program we set up last year to get men and women back to work? All sorts of useful and helpful projects are being accomplished because of this program, so I would urge your Aunt Dora to apply at your local office as soon as possible.

Very sincerely yours,

Franklin D. Roosevelt

To learn more about families on relief, visit winslowpress.com.

North Adams, Massachusetts

Dear Mr. President Roosevelt,

I told my Aunt Dora what you said about the WPA. She went down to that office, and they told her they're only taking people from the relief rolls. That seems crazy to me. It seems like the people who don't want to work are the ones getting jobs. The Italian people are very proud because we've been working hard to stay off the relief. So she's mad about that.

Tony says to tell you that he's been doing lots of projects.

They fixed up a dam, they stopped those gypsy moths from eating all the leaves, and they thinned out lots of little trees. Here is the list of all the trees they planted this spring: white ash, beech, sugar maple, white birch, yellow birch, red maple, and yellow poplar. Now, when we walk up the hill to Witt's Ledge, he tells me which tree is which. I still can't see no difference, so I don't know if he's right or not.

Your friend,

Emma Bartoletti

Emma Bartoletti

Inset: CCC workers in Beltsville, Maryland, 1935.
Background: A stand of Scotch pine thinned by young men in the CCC

July 24, 1936

Hyde Park, New York

Dear Emma,

I do understand how frustrated your Aunt Dora must be at not getting a job with the WPA. But think how hard it is for people on the relief rolls. Just because they have had to take money from the government does not mean that they don't want to work as much as all of you do. I have heard recently from the WPA administrator that some of the rules for eligibility will soon be changed to include people like Aunt Dora. Tell her to keep checking. A huge government program like this is always difficult to administer efficiently, but we are doing our best.

Tell Tony how proud I am of the work he is doing. From my bed in Hyde Park, I look out into the branches of an enormous yellow poplar tree. It is one of the most soothing and inspiring views that I know of. The next time he takes you on a walk, see if he can find you a yellow poplar so you'll know what it looks like.

Your friend,

Franklin D. Roosevelt

Franklin D. Roosevelt

Springwood, the Roosevelts' house in Hyde Park, New York

August 12, 1936

North Adams, Massachusetts
Dear Mr. President Roosevelt,

Guess who came to North Adams yesterday? Babe Ruth. That's right. He came with the Brooklyn Dodgers to play the Sons of Italy team, and the camp let Tony off. He got to pitch to Babe Ruth in the fourth! How about that?

The manager of the Sons of Italy team got the Brooklyn Dodgers to come up and play one of those games against them. I can't remember the name, and I'm too excited to look it up in the dictionary. I think it starts with a XZ. Xzibishun or something. And Babe Ruth came, too. It was raining yesterday morning, and the field was soaking wet. People were saying maybe they couldn't play the game. The Bambino and the rest of the team were coming in on the 3:21 Minuteman train, so a lot of the men went down to the lumberyard and loaded up a truck with sawdust. They spread it over the field and poured gasoline on it and lit it on fire. You should have seen the flames. We kids were just getting out of school, and we were running over to the depot to see the train get in when suddenly the whole field blew up into flames. The fire department was already there, but nothing bad happened and the field got dried out enough, which is what they meant to do.

The train pulled in on time. When Babe came down the steps, we yelled and screamed and jumped up and down. Babe picked up one of the little boys and carried him for a block or so on his shoulders. Tony told me to get the Babe's autograph because he wasn't coming down from the camp till game time. So I pushed right to the front and ran along next to him. I was the only girl up there. Maybe that's why

 To learn more about Babe Ruth, visit winslowpress.com.

Background: A baseball game, c. 1936

he picked me. He took the baseball and signed it for me, and I told him my brother Tony might be pitching against him later. He laughed and patted me on the shoulder. He's a big man. He's bigger than he looks in the newspaper pictures. He looks kind of tired and sad, like maybe baseball and all those home runs just wore him out.

Tony rode in on the CCC truck with the other guys from the camp. People came to the game from all over. The papers say 3,000 people were there. They say it's the biggest crowd that ever watched a baseball game in North Adams. We went early to watch batting practice. At the start of the game, the whole crowd rose and took off their hats while the Sons of Italy band played the Star Spangled Banner. It was INSPIRING.

Our team was winning all the way to the seventh inning. They let Tony pitch in the fourth, and Babe was put out on a pop fly. The crowd was yelling at Tony to lay the ball right in there so Babe could hit a home run in North Adams. But even though Tony did it, Babe didn't connect. They pulled Tony out in the fifth to let someone else pitch. The Dodgers won 6 to 2, but our team didn't have any errors, and we got nine hits against major-league pitchers. How about that?

You should have been there.

Your friend,

Emma Bartoletti

Emma Bartoletti

The White House, Washington, D.C.

Dear Emma,

I wish I could have been there to see Tony pitch to the Sultan of Swat. The word you were looking for is "exhibition." Good thing you didn't waste time looking under the Z's.

I've begun my campaign for the November elections, and am off tomorrow for a tour through North Carolina and Tennessee. I do greatly miss the advice and companionship of my good friend Louis Howe, who died in April, but I've asked Mrs. R. to step in and help, and she has done much to organize the forces at Democratic headquarters.

Four years ago we had a hear-nothing, see-nothing, do-nothing government. I believe the great majority of Americans recognize how much has changed since then and will vote their convictions. My job is simply to remind them every so often of the way things used to be, when so few people held so much economic power. One of the most irritating things is the way the newspaper editors are aligned against our policies even though most of their reporters write in sympathy with our cause. I expect you will find this to be true if you look at the editorial pages of your *North Adams Transcript*.

Very truly yours,

Franklin D. Roosevelt

September 7, 1936

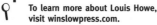

To learn more about Louis Howe, visit winslowpress.com.

A close-up of FDR's face

September 15, 1936

North Adams, Massachusetts
Dear Mr. President Roosevelt,

Okay, I see that the WPA is a good thing. They transferred Mr. Gaioni over to it from his old ERA job and now he's working on the Notch Road that goes up to the top of Mount Greylock. I know what you're going to say. He's Italian and he went on relief. He's got six children to feed. And a sickly wife who don't work. So some Italians go on relief. Maybe just not Bartolettis and Covellos.

Tony's camp had a party at the state armory in Adams, and the WPA brought in the vaudeville acts. I didn't know the WPA did things like that. We went up there to watch, and it was funny. The WPA also had an EXHIBITION in the library. Aunt Dora made me go with her. I thought it was boring. There were a lot of old newspapers and pictures and clothes about the start of the town. The WPA is paying for the library to make a list of all the books they have, and then they've got to glue up some of the ripped ones. The librarian is a friend of Aunt Dora's, so maybe she can get her one of those jobs.

We've got the biggest list of people who want to vote ever in the city of North Adams. I hope they all vote Democratic, but I can't promise you nothing because you don't come near here. Mr. Landon was down in Pittsfield last night talking off the back of a train. The newspaper said that 5,000 people went to hear him. So I hope you come here pretty soon to tell everybody that those Republicans are a bunch of sneaky rich people and they shouldn't get fooled by them. You're right about the *Transcript*. We don't ever read the editorial page because it makes us so mad. Besides that, they don't list the times for masses at St. Anthony's Church, and they

To learn more about the Works Progress Administration, visit winslowpress.com.

An election cartoon by Clifford Berryman, c. 1936

list all the other church services in town. My father says that's because our church is Italian and the *Transcript* is run by Yankees who don't like it that so many foreigners have moved to North Adams. Don't you wish that people could just get along with each other even if they started out in different countries?

I began ninth grade at Drury High School. Me and that boy named Felix formed the Drury Democrats, so we're doing what we can to get you elected. We go around in the Italian neighborhood and pass out papers about you and make sure everybody is signed up to vote.

I pray that you'll win. I think that's important enough for the Virgin Mary to pay attention. I sure don't think she'd want that Mr. Landon.

Your friend,

Emma Bartoletti

Emma Bartoletti

P.S. We're back to rooting for the Yankees. I think Babe Ruth would like that. He told the *Transcript* he thinks the Yankees are going to win the pennant this year. With Joe DiMaggio on the team added to Tony Lazzeri and Frank Crosetti, that makes three Italians. One third of the team, Tony says.

October 4, 1936

Hyde Park, New York

Dear Emma,

I am sending along this program from the second game of the World Series for you and Tony. I was lucky enough to be at the Polo Grounds for that game and saw your friend Tony Lazzeri hit a grand slam in the third inning. That certainly blew the game wide open and rattled those Giants. He almost did it again with that fifth inning drive to center field. Too bad Leiber pulled it down at the last minute. And Joe DiMaggio caught a long fly off Leiber to end the game. He was still standing there when my car drove through the centerfield gate, and I gave him the high sign from you and your brother. He waved back at me.

I'm trying to get up to New England for another campaign swing, but I figure with Emma Bartoletti signed on as my campaign manager, I'd better pay some attention to the Midwest. So in a few days I am off to visit Illinois, Iowa (I'll say hello to Dubuque for Tony), Nebraska, Wyoming, Colorado, Kansas (where Mr. Landon comes from), Missouri, Michigan, Ohio, and New York. It promises to be a whirlwind tour, but I am looking forward to getting out of Washington and hearing what everyday Americans have to say about the state of the country.

And yes, I do wish people would get along with each other no matter what color their skin or what language they speak. I don't mind a good argument once in a while when people don't agree on how to solve a problem, but prejudice is something the world could certainly do without.

Yours very truly,

Franklin D. Roosevelt

Franklin D. Roosevelt

FDR talking to a group of men while campaigning in Mandan, North Dakota, 1936

North Adams, Massachusetts

Dear Mr. President Roosevelt,

Tony really liked the program from the World Series. Me too. He wanted to take it up to the camp but I wouldn't let him. Somebody might of stole it up there. We're keeping it next to the ball Babe Ruth signed.

Now the Bartoletti family got good news again. My mother got a five percent raise. She's making $14.20. And my Aunt Dora got a job with that WPA. She's teaching adult aliens at night school five nights a week and Saturdays, too. That means she's got Italians and French Canadians and Irish and Polish and all sorts of other new immigrants trying to learn English. It's too late for this election, but I told her they all got to vote for you when they get to be citizens. She says she can't tell them that. I don't know why she can't. At least they got to be Democrats.

We had fireworks for Columbus Day down on Noel Field. That's the same place where Babe Ruth came to play, the one we can see from my house. (They used to call it State Street Field, but then it got named after some famous dead man who liked sports and teams.) We can see everything from Aunt Ida's porch so we had a party up there and lots of people came to watch. That was a good thing, because it was freezing and windy and the people down on the field must of been pretty cold.

Too bad you couldn't get no closer than Worcester when you came through here this week. Your speech was pretty good. I liked that you said "people are more important than machines." I told Felix you must have got that idea from my mother.

I wish I was old enough to vote.

Your friend,

Emma Bartoletti

Emma Bartoletti

October 29, 1936

The White House, Washington, D.C.

Dear Emma,

I wish you could vote, too. A few more Emma Bartolettis, and I think we'd have this one in the bag.

Sorry I have no time to write a longer letter. I'm just back from a trip through Pennsylvania and Delaware, and my desk is piled high with papers I must attend to.

Very truly yours,

Franklin D. Roosevelt

Franklin D. Roosevelt

The wear and tear of the presidential office is beginning to show on FDR's face in this photo.

North Adams, Massachusetts

Dear Mr. President Roosevelt,

Here is the report from your Campaign Manager. North Adams went 6,085 for Roosevelt and 3,468 for Landon. I bet half of those voters were Italians. And Pittsfield went 11,272 for you and 8,310 for Landon. So I guess Mr. Landon didn't change too many people's minds when he come to town. Even Mr. Landon's cousin who goes to the fancy college in the next town said he was voting for you.

I warned you about Vermont, Mr. President Roosevelt. But just like I said before, Readsboro went for you. Lots of Northern Italians up there.

Felix and Natalie and I are putting out a special report from the Drury Democrats about the election. We've been very busy.

My HEARTIEST CONGRATULATIONS. I wish you CONTINUED SUCCESS in your president business.

Your Italian-American friend,

Emma Bartoletti

Emma Bartoletti

 To learn more about Alf M. Landon and the election of 1936, visit winslowpress.com.

109

December 21, 1936

The White House, Washington, D.C.

Dear Emma,

Thank you for delivering North Adams into the Roosevelt column. I sincerely hope I will be able to live up to your trust in me.

I wish you and your family the happiest of Christmases, and enclose my usual present. What with your letters to me and your homework and your special reports, the question of paper shortage must have grown acute.

As always, I plan to read *A Christmas Carol* by Charles Dickens to our assembled friends and family on Christmas Eve, and I enclose a copy of the book for you to enjoy. I highly recommend it. Like the reformed Mr. Scrooge, I hope to keep the spirit of Christmas alive all through the year. Let's pray that the mill owners and the other businessmen do the same!

Yours very sincerely,

Franklin D. Roosevelt

Four generations of Roosevelts and friends gather for a Christmas photo at the White House.

North Adams, Massachusetts
Dear Mr. President Roosevelt,

February 1, 1937

I went to your birthday party last Saturday night in the State Armory. My mother and father bought the tickets for me and Aunt Dora. They say 6,000 towns all over the country are giving you a birthday party. Mr. Wall ADMINISTERED the one in North Adams. He gave a speech about how much money we were giving to stop infantile paralysis in North Adams. He talked about the boy in Adams who died last week. That boy had been living in an iron lung for a year. Some of the money we are sending to your place in Georgia. I hope they find a cure for that disease soon.

When you started speaking on the radio, everybody stopped their dancing to listen. When you were done, everybody sang you happy birthday. The Italians all stood together and we sang you *buon compleanno*. That's "happy birthday" in Italian.

Thank you for the paper. We are using it all the time. Also for the book. I read it aloud to my family, and at first, Maria Angela was scared by the ghost. But she liked Tiny Tim a lot.

My father got a raise from Arnold Print Works last week. Now he makes $18 a week. The Bartoletti family is okay for now.

Your friend,

Emma Bartoletti

Emma Bartoletti

FDR's Fireside Chats could be heard on battery-operated radios like this one.

Franklin D. Roosevelt: Historical Notes

1900

Enters Harvard
University. Father
dies three
months into his
first year.

More about Franklin D. Roosevelt

At the end of the twentieth century, President Bill Clinton
offered up his thoughts: "When our children's children read
the story of the twentieth century, they will see that above all,
it is the story of freedom's triumph: the victory of democracy
over fascism and totalitarianism; of free enterprise over
command economies; of tolerance over bigotry. And they will
see that the embodiment of that triumph, the driving force
behind it, was President Franklin Delano Roosevelt."

This is the man who led the United States, and at times the
entire world, through times of crisis: the Depression and
World War II. President Franklin D. Roosevelt was in office
for twelve years, longer than any other U.S. president. He
was elected to four terms. He became president during the
deepest economic depression the United States has ever
known, and died in office after leading the country through
World War II. FDR, as he was called, made those he led feel
confident. Eleanor Roosevelt once said of him, "I've never
known a man who gave one a greater sense of security." He
was a calming presence in the midst of panic-stricken times.
He believed his role as president was "to preserve under the
changing conditions of each generation a people's government
for the people's good."

FDR was known and loved for his desire to create
opportunities for the common people of the United States
during a period in which many were suffering from the

FDR on his yacht at Campobello Island, Canada

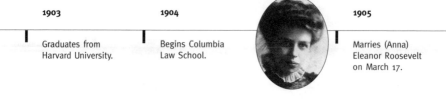

1903	1904		1905
Graduates from Harvard University.	Begins Columbia Law School.		Marries (Anna) Eleanor Roosevelt on March 17.

Depression. Yet this man who was committed to fighting for the common people of the United States was in fact from a wealthy, aristocratic family.

Early Life

Franklin was born on January 30, 1882, the only son of Sara Delano and James Roosevelt, a wealthy railroad executive. He was raised under the care of his doting mother at Hyde Park, the family property in the Hudson Valley of New York. Until he was fourteen years of age, Franklin was taught by tutors and private governesses, which made it easier for him to travel with his parents for months at a time. Because of this, however, he lived his early life away from children of his own age. When he attended school at Groton, a boarding school in Massachusetts, he found it difficult to adjust to the social life. Franklin wanted to be liked more than anything, yet he did not fit in. Years later, as FDR was gaining public attention through politics, a fellow Groton classmate commented that he did not understand what others saw in Franklin.

As Franklin entered Harvard University, he strove to become popular. Although he did not excel in his grades, he developed a charm that attracted others. He worked on the college newspaper and won offices frequently. Franklin was not an exceptional student, but he was ambitious. This was due partly to the influence of his role model, his fifth cousin and the president of the United States, Theodore Roosevelt. Franklin deeply admired the president. He structured his route to the

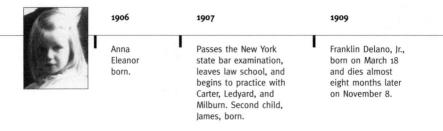

presidency after Theodore's, and he once named him the greatest man he ever knew.

Franklin formed another link to Theodore during his college years when he began to date Theodore's niece, Eleanor Roosevelt. She was Franklin's distant cousin, and on the surface the two appeared very different. Eleanor was shy and serious. She viewed herself as an ugly duckling, in part because she lacked a nurturing family. Her parents had died when she was young, leaving her to be raised by her severe grandmother. Franklin had emerged by this time as a handsome, sociable, and popular personality. Eleanor's desire for social justice attracted him. She introduced him to the tenements in the lower east side of New York City, where she had been doing volunteer work. Franklin gave Eleanor stability and a hope of intimacy that she had not known at home. While their marriage was difficult and at times disappointing to both, they formed a political partnership that made history for its strength and sense of purpose. They changed the nation through their commitment to reform for the people of the United States. Their partnership began when the two were married on March 17, 1905. President Theodore Roosevelt gave Eleanor away, which made the wedding a national event.

Franklin's mother had disapproved of the marriage, and although Franklin respected her opinion, he remained steadfast about marrying Eleanor. After the marriage, Franklin's mother dictated where the young couple should live and assumed the role of woman of the house. In the early

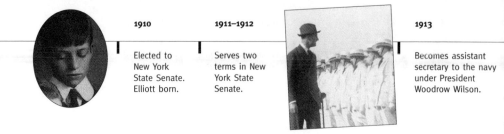

1910
Elected to New York State Senate. Elliott born.

1911–1912
Serves two terms in New York State Senate.

1913
Becomes assistant secretary to the navy under President Woodrow Wilson.

years of marriage, Eleanor submitted to her mother-in-law's wishes. In her autobiography, *This Is My Story*, she writes: "I left everything to my mother-in-law and my husband. I was growing dependent on my mother-in-law, requiring her help on almost every subject."

Franklin and Eleanor had six children in the first ten years of their marriage—Anna, James, Franklin (who died at eight months), Elliot, Franklin Delano, Jr., and John. Tending to the children was Eleanor's role in the family, while Franklin attended law school long enough to pass the bar exam and begin a career as a lawyer.

Early Career

Practicing law held little joy for Franklin, so after four years he entered the world of politics. While Franklin admired Theodore Roosevelt, a Republican, his own father was a Democrat. Franklin also knew that as a Republican, he would be competing with Theodore's sons for candidacy. As a Democrat, the Roosevelt name would work for his benefit without any family competition. Although Franklin was politically inexperienced, he had the name and the wealth to support a campaign. The state convention nominated Franklin as a Democratic candidate for the New York State Senate in 1910.

He quickly gained attention in Albany, the capital of New York, because of his progressive ideas and his fight against Tammany Hall politics. Tammany Hall, the executive com-

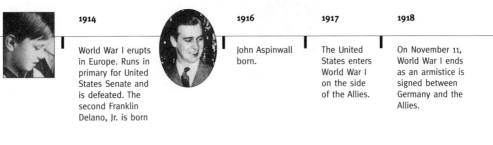

1914	1916	1917	1918
World War I erupts in Europe. Runs in primary for United States Senate and is defeated. The second Franklin Delano, Jr. is born	John Aspinwall born.	The United States enters World War I on the side of the Allies.	On November 11, World War I ends as an armistice is signed between Germany and the Allies.

mittee of the Democratic party in New York City, exercised strong control over the Democrats. Franklin stood up against Tammany and encouraged others to do the same, which cost him the U.S. Senate seat in 1914. He was accused of snobbery and high-class airs, so he worked hard at relating to the common man. He fought to improve the agricultural needs of his own county, as well as for conservation. Franklin loved nature and especially the sea, and often spoke out in favor of legislation to protect it. Despite the opposition from Tammany, Franklin was considered a strong representative for his county in the Senate, and was re-elected in 1912.

During his second term as a state senator, FDR supported Woodrow Wilson's presidential campaign. When Wilson was elected president, he appointed FDR assistant secretary of the navy. Because of Roosevelt's enthusiasm for the navy as well as his desire to learn politically, this position suited him well. He was a headstrong assistant and often came into conflict with his boss, the secretary of the navy, Josephus Daniels. FDR had a good relationship with the officers of the navy, while Daniels did not. Yet during this time, FDR learned both the wisdom of Daniels's ways with politicians and the administrative side of politics necessary for higher political positions.

In 1914, FDR sought the New York Democratic nomination for U.S. senator. Tammany opposed him, and FDR lost. Roosevelt discovered that he could not alienate such a strong force in New York politics and still hope to win a major

1920

Runs as vice president
with James Cox in
presidential election
and is defeated.

1921

On August 10,
contracts polio
and never walks
unaided again.

1928

Elected governor
of New York.

election. In later years, Franklin worked with progressive
Tammany politicians to form a friendlier relationship. In
time, Tammany was able to forgive and support FDR in his
politics. In the meantime, Franklin continued as assistant
secretary of the navy. In 1917, when the tensions were high
between the U.S. and Germany, Franklin went to President
Wilson to urge that the navy be readied for action. Wilson told
him: "I want history to show not only that we have tried every
diplomatic means to keep out of the war; to show that war has
been forced upon us deliberately by Germany; but also that
we have come into the court of history with clean hands."
Roosevelt would remember these words before the U.S.
entered World War II. President Wilson taught Roosevelt
the importance of avoiding war whenever possible.

Once the U.S. was in the war, Roosevelt wanted to join the
armed forces, but Wilson and Daniels wanted to keep him in
Washington, D.C. Franklin remained the assistant secretary of
the navy until 1920, when he was chosen as the Democratic
vice-presidential nominee with James M. Cox, the governor
of Ohio. Roosevelt again worked hard on the campaign and
was well received, but the American public was ready for a
change from Wilson's administration and elected Harding
and Coolidge. Roosevelt returned to his law career in New
York. He formed a law firm, but was interrupted within a
year by a personal crisis. In fact, two major crises arose in the
Roosevelt family during the years following World War I.

First, in 1918, Eleanor came upon some love letters written

The stock market crashes
on October 29, beginning
the Great Depression.

Reelected governor
of New York.

Elected as 32nd
president of the
United States.

to Franklin from Eleanor's social secretary, Lucy Mercer. Eleanor was devastated. Her hopes for an intimate marriage were shattered. Eleanor offered Franklin a divorce. He refused; a divorce would have thwarted his presidential ambitions. At this time in history, and in the Roosevelts' social class, a divorce was unacceptable. Eleanor demanded that if she were to remain in the marriage, he never see Lucy Mercer again. Despite Franklin's agreement and decision to honor her request, the intimacy of their relationship was never restored. Eleanor developed her own political career, causes, and travel schedule. She spoke out in favor of civil rights, women's rights, and the underprivileged. Although she remained a political partner to FDR, she led her own active life apart from Franklin's.

The second crisis for the Roosevelts, and especially for Franklin, was his contraction of infantile paralysis, also known as polio, a dreaded disease that left him unable to walk on his own. The symptoms appeared in August of 1921, after he went swimming at Campobello, the island in New Brunswick, Canada, where he and his family often spent vacations. He spent the next seven years of his life working to recover from the disease. Franklin was determined to regain the use of his legs. While his mother thought he should retire to a life of leisure in the country, Eleanor encouraged him to return to politics. During his recuperation, Eleanor and Louis Howe, a close friend and political adviser, actively spoke in his name, keeping his presence alive in the political realm.

1933

On March 4, inaugurated as president. On March 9, declares a national bank holiday and calls an emergency meeting of Congress, which begins "The Hundred Days" of "The New Deal."

1935

Establishes the Works Progress Administration (WPA), National Youth Administration (NYA), and other programs of the New Deal.

Franklin, aware that his physical condition could negatively impact public opinion, did not allow the severity of his illness to be known. This continued throughout his presidency. He was rarely photographed in a wheelchair, and never when he was being carried. It was not widely known how severely polio had affected his legs until after his death.

Franklin tried hard to conceal his physical pain. Although walking or standing could be extremely painful for him, he learned to maintain a cheerful, relaxed expression in order to disguise his handicap. He did not want the public to question his strength or ability to perform the duties of his position.

It is important to note that while Franklin hid his physical condition from the general public, he was not ashamed of the polio. Eleanor noted that "probably the thing that took most courage in his life was his mastery and his meeting of polio…he just accepted it as one of those things that was given you as discipline in life." Others who worked alongside him and knew him well thought that the polio had taught Franklin humility and compassion toward others. The pain and suffering had brought a depth to him that some thought he had previously lacked. It was through Franklin that the National Foundation for Infantile Paralysis, an organization established to find a cure for polio, was founded in 1938. Franklin also bought Warm Springs, a health resort in Georgia, in order to provide a place for polio victims to visit for therapy.

1936	1938	1939

| Reelected president. | Germany, under Adolf Hitler, invades Austria and part of Czechoslovakia. | World War II begins as Germany invades Poland in September and the Allies declare war on Germany |

Roosevelt as Governor

Roosevelt did not allow polio to destroy his life. In 1928, Franklin began the campaign for governor of New York. Again, he campaigned well, traveling in a car driven by hand controls. Roosevelt won the election by a narrow margin, yet for him it was a triumphant return to politics.

As governor, Roosevelt fought for conservation, agricultural, and labor reforms. FDR wanted to limit the hours women and children could work. He was aware that farmers were struggling financially, and tried to gain lower taxes for them. He was an effective administrator and popular with the citizens of New York.

In October of 1929, the stock market crashed. The economy of the nation began to fall apart. Agriculture and construction especially were in financial trouble. At first, Roosevelt proposed only limited help to those who were unemployed, since unemployment was not widespread. As the crash began to ripple through the nation's economy, however, unemployment continued to rise. Roosevelt kept a close watch on conditions and learned as much as he could from economic experts. When the ripple effects began to devastate the nation in 1931, Roosevelt pushed the government to act quickly to provide relief. He founded relief organizations that provided ten percent of New York families with enough money to prevent them from starving. The Great Depression had hit the United States.

In 1930, in the midst of the effects of the stock market

1940

FDR reelected to a third term
as president. France falls to the
Axis powers.

1941

Japan attacks the United States on
December 7 at Hawaii's Pearl Harbor
navy and air base. U.S. declares war
on Japan, and three days later, on
Germany and Italy.

crash, Roosevelt ran for a second term as governor. His goal was not only to win the election, but also to win by enough votes to be the obvious choice for the Democratic presidential nominee in the next two years. Roosevelt won by such a landslide that newspaper reporter Will Rogers wrote the next day, "The Democrats nominated their President yesterday, Franklin D. Roosevelt."

The Road to the Presidency

The nomination for the presidency was not so easy. At the convention, Roosevelt held the lead among the Democrats for the nomination, but he could not get enough votes until another candidate, John Nance Garner, backed out when promised the vice presidential nomination. At this point, Roosevelt broke a precedent by flying to the convention in order to promise the Democrats, "I pledge you, I pledge myself, to a new deal for the American people. . . . Give me your help, not to win votes alone, but to win in this crusade to restore America to its own people."

Roosevelt campaigned across the country, speaking out in support of farmers, federal relief, old-age pensions, and conservation reforms. The people of the United States were scared and weary from the extensive Depression. Roosevelt's promises were vague, but worth a try, and so the American people elected Franklin D. Roosevelt by a margin of 22,815,539 popular votes to Hoover's 15,750,000. FDR carried 42 of the 48 states, with 472 electoral votes to Hoover's 59.

In April, Lieutenant Doolittle leads bombing raid on Tokyo. Admiral Nimitz and General Eisenhower lead the U.S. to retake the Philippines. In November, the Allies invade North Africa.

The Allies defeat Germany in North Africa and invade Italy. FDR, Churchill, and Stalin meet at Tehran, Iran, to plan the Allied invasion of France.

The Presidency during the Depression

Franklin D. Roosevelt became the 32nd president of the United States on March 4, 1933. At this time, between 13 and 15 million Americans were unemployed. Banks were in serious trouble. Roosevelt called an emergency meeting of Congress on March 9 and pronounced a national bank holiday, which froze the banks until Congress could legislate emergency financial support. This accomplished, three fourths of the banks were able to reopen permanently. With Congress ready to support his reforms, FDR introduced more programs. Congress remained in session for what was known as "The Hundred Days." It produced more legislation with lasting effects in that amount of time than has any other session of Congress before or since.

FDR began attacking the Depression by establishing "The New Deal." He established programs to provide work for the unemployed. The Civilian Conservation Corps (CCC) was one of his favorites. This gave young men between the ages of eighteen and twenty-five the chance to work in state and federal parks, improving the land. From 1933 until its completion in 1942, 2 million men were employed by the government, building roads, planting trees, and reducing the effects of floods and other natural disasters. FDR introduced projects that restored the land and at the same time trained the young men who worked it.

The Tennessee Valley Authority (TVA) built dams to control flooding as well as harness useful energy. The National

The Allies' invasion of France begins on the beaches of Normandy on June 6. FDR is reelected to a fourth term in spite of failing health. Senator Harry Truman is his vice-presidential running mate.

Recovery Administration (NRA) regulated minimum wages, working hours, and pricing. It was less effective than Roosevelt had hoped, however, and was declared unconstitutional by the Supreme Court in 1935. The Agricultural Adjustment Administration (AAA) regulated the production of farmers in order to cut back on the surplus and raise prices.

The Works Progress Administration (WPA) was established in 1935 to get more Americans back to work. It was successful, paying as much as $11 billion to 3.2 million Americans a month. The purpose of this program was to employ professionals in their fields as well as provide work to unskilled workers. Thus, artists painted murals on public buildings; photographers, such as Dorothea Lange, photographed migrant workers; writers authored travel books for areas within the United States; and construction workers built much-needed bridges and highways. La Guardia Airport in New York City, for example, was one of the many public projects built under the WPA.

By 1935, FDR's initial confidence and his emergency measures were slowing down. Yet his programs had brought such relief that the American public reelected Roosevelt in 1936, again with a substantial victory. He carried forty-six of forty-eight states.

During his second term, Roosevelt hit the lowest point of his presidency. He tried to increase the number of Supreme Court justices from nine to fifteen in order to appoint six more justices. Congress opposed him in this attempt. Strikes

FDR, Churchill, and Stalin meet in Yalta, USSR to discuss final attack and postwar plans. Upon returning to U.S., FDR's failing health sends him to Warm Springs, Georgia, where he dies on April 12 at the age of 63. Truman is inaugurated as 33rd president of the United States. Victory in Europe (V-E) Day on May 8 signals the end of the war in Europe. The Allies drop two atomic bombs on Japan, which surrenders on August 14. World War II ends.

broke out among labor, and conservatives blamed Roosevelt for causing them. Cutbacks in government spending led to a recession in the fall of 1937, shattering hopes that the country was moving out of the Depression. Roosevelt asked for increased spending in 1938 in order to counter the new recession that was again sweeping the country.

Throughout the 1930s, trouble was also brewing abroad. Germany was gaining power under the leadership of Adolf Hitler. Italy and Japan were also rising in power, and the three eventually came together to form the Axis Powers. The Allied countries, especially Britain and France, became increasingly uncomfortable with Germany's growing power and aggressiveness. As Hitler broke pact after pact, European tensions intensified and France declared war on Germany following Germany's invasion of Poland in 1939.

Roosevelt was not as neutral concerning the war as the American people were, yet he did not feel that he could actively help the Allies without the support of the country, which wanted no part of a European war. Many European countries had not repaid their debt to the United States from the first World War. The situation became desperate as Hitler invaded Austria and part of Czechoslovakia in 1938, Poland in 1939, then Holland, Luxembourg, Denmark, Belgium, and finally France in 1940. Roosevelt began to work out a way to support Britain by establishing Lend-Lease, a policy that allowed Britain to receive supplies from the United States, occasionally under U.S. escort. This lend-lease policy was extended to the Soviet Union in 1941, after Germany declared war on the Soviets. Still, the American people wanted to remain neutral.

While Hitler was the aggressor in Europe, Japan invaded China in 1937. Roosevelt attempted to contain the invasion, by imposing an embargo to prevent Japan from moving into Indochina. During 1936, another presidential election was under way. Roosevelt's second term had not been as successful as his first, and many people, including Democratic leaders, were opposed to Roosevelt's running for a third term. The American people did not want war, and both candidates promised that they would not enter the war. Roosevelt stated specifically that he would not send American boys across the sea to fight. Critics have accused him of misleading the country. They believed that at this point he knew the United States could not remain neutral for long. Still he promised that he would not be the first to attack or send troops to fight for another country. He did remain true to his promise, and the United States did not commit troops abroad until Japan attacked Pearl Harbor.

The American people elected Roosevelt to an unprecedented third term. This margin was much less: 27,243,466 to 22,334,413 in the popular vote, and 449 to 82 in electoral votes.

The Presidency during the War

Japan, after trying to extend its reach into Southeast Asia, was angered when America imposed an embargo. Japan, an ally of Germany and Italy, retaliated by attacking America's naval and air base, Pearl Harbor in Hawaii, on December 7, 1941. Few American leaders had anticipated that Hawaii would be a target for a Japanese attack. This mistake was devastating to the navy, the American people, and especially to Roosevelt himself. Eight American battleships and thirteen other navy ships were either sunk or seriously damaged. Three thousand five hundred men were killed or wounded. The attack and its devastation shocked the American people into unifying against the enemy. The U.S. declared war on Japan and three days later, on Germany and Italy. Winston Churchill, the prime minister of Britain, was elated. Now Britain would no longer have to stand alone against the enemy.

Germany and Italy declared war on the United States, and the European war quickly expanded into World War II. Roosevelt had already established a peacetime draft, registering all men between the ages of twenty-one and thirty-five. Sixteen million men registered. Factories began to produce massive amounts of military supplies. Women worked where men had left vacancies. War production finally brought the United States out of its decade of depression.

While Japan was slowly taking over Southeast Asia, the Allied forces focused on Germany and Italy. In 1942, however, the Allies began to attack Japanese holdings. Lieutenant Doolittle led a daring raid on Tokyo. Admiral Nimitz and General MacArthur reacquired the Philippines, which became an important link to the east and a military base for Allied forces. Also in 1942 Lieutenant General Eisenhower attacked North Africa in order to break into Europe by way of Italy. By 1943, Allied forces were able to invade Italy.

In 1943, Roosevelt, Winston Churchill of Britain, and Joseph Stalin of the Soviet Union met in Tehran, Iran, to plan the invasion of Normandy, France. German leaders knew the Allies would invade the western coast of France, but could only speculate as to where on the vast coastline the invasion would take place. After many months of planning, the Allied forces landed on the beaches of Normandy with the largest naval force ever gathered. Early in the morning on June 6, 1944, paratroopers began what would be remembered as "The Longest Day" by landing in France before dawn. German forces were shocked to see ship after ship emerging from the fog to land on the beaches. General Eisenhower led the attack, in which 9,000 ships and 11,000 aircraft penetrated the well-defended French coastline. German anti-invasion tactics inflicted heavy casualties on Allied troops, but the invasion was the beginning of the end for Germany.

Nineteen forty-four was again a presidential election year. Roosevelt's health was failing. His heart was weak and he tired easily, but he was not confident that another candidate could win both an election and a war. He reluctantly ran for a fourth term, hiding his physical condition from the public. Franklin's advisers suspected that he would not live through the term, and encouraged him to take on Senator Harry Truman as his vice presidential candidate. Again, the election was close, yet Roosevelt and Truman won, with 25,612,474 to 22,017,570 in popular votes and 432 to 99 in electoral votes.

In February 1945, Roosevelt met with Stalin and Churchill, this time at Yalta in the Soviet Union. They discussed the final attack on Germany and postwar plans. Many critics believed that Roosevelt's failing health caused him to grant Stalin too much power over Eastern Europe. Upon his return to the United States, Roosevelt traveled to Warm Springs to recuperate. He never recovered, however, and died on April 12, 1945, an exhausted man who had borne the weight of a country for twelve years. Hitler and Mussolini both died in that same month, and Victory in Europe (V-E Day) was achieved on May 8, 1945, within a month of Roosevelt's death.

The war with Japan continued until President Harry Truman ordered two atomic bombs to be dropped on strategic cities rather than risk the Allied lives necessary for a land invasion. The atomic bombs devastated the Japanese people, causing more than 200,000 deaths and burns from radiation. Japan surrendered on August 14, 1945, ending World War II.

The funeral of Franklin D. Roosevelt took place in Washington, D.C., on April 14, 1945. His body was then taken to Hyde Park, his family home in New York.

Franklin D. Roosevelt has been a controversial president for years. Historians debate his success during the Depression and his foreign policy before and during the war. Yet he succeeded in passing legislation which would protect the country from experiencing another paralyzing depression. He brought about programs and reforms that still support the common people, such as a minimum wage and Social Security. He led the country through a world war equal to no other. Most importantly, Franklin Roosevelt inspired a weary, scared, and hopeless people.

Books written for kids

Freedman, Russell. *Franklin Delano Roosevelt*. New York: Clarion Books, 1990.

Meltzer, Milton. *Brother, Can You Spare a Dime: The Great Depression of 1929-1933*. New York: Facts on File, 1990.

Morris, Jeffrey. *The FDR Way (Great Presidential Decisions)*. Minneapolis: Lerner Publications Company, 1996.

Nardo, Don. *Franklin D. Roosevelt: U.S. President (Great Achievers: Lives of the Physically Challenged)*. New York: Chelsea House Publishers, 1996.

Osinski, Alice. *Franklin D. Roosevelt: Encyclopedia of Presidents*. Chicago: Children's Press, 1987.

Books written for adults

Alsop, Joseph. *FDR, 1882-1945: The Life and Times of Franklin D. Roosevelt*. New York: Gramercy Books, an imprint of Random House, 1998.

Davis, Kenneth S. *FDR, The New Deal Years: 1933-37, A History*. New York: Random House, 1986.

Freidel, Frank. *Franklin D. Roosevelt: A Rendezvous with Destiny*. Boston: Little, Brown and Company, 1990.

Goodwin, Doris Kearns. *No Ordinary Time*. New York: Simon & Schuster, 1994.

Larsen, Rebecca. *Franklin D. Roosevelt: Man of Destiny*. New York: Franklin Watts, 1991.

Lash, Joseph. *Eleanor and Franklin: The Story of Their Relationship*. New York: Norton, 1971.

Roosevelt, Elliott. *As He Saw It*. New York: Duell, Sloan and Pearce, 1946.

Audio tapes and books that kids and adults can enjoy

FDR: Nothing to Fear: Featuring Speeches Given by Franklin Delano Roosevelt by Franklin Delano Roosevelt (Reader).

Roosevelt, Franklin Delano; John Grafton (editor), *Great Speeches*. New York: Dover Publications, 1999.

Here is a reproduction of an actual letter from Franklin Delano
Roosevelt to Eleanor Roosevelt, written on November 17, 1933.

Emma Bartoletti's letters might have looked something like this:

September 13, 1933

Dear Mr. President Roosevelt,
Last week, my father was making $20 a week and now he only gonna be making $14. He says you are a president and you know best, but I'm not so sure about that. So please explain to me what you are thinking.
Your friend,
Emma Bartoletti

By the time the correspondence in this book takes place, the United States Postal Service was a well-organized and highly developed department in the government, but it was also about to face the Depression along with the rest of the country. In the years leading up to the Depression, the Post Office progressed with the times, using new modes of transportation and also developing the public service philosophy for which it became known.

The Post Office handled more than 27 million pieces of mail of all kinds per year during the late 1920s and early 1930s. In the years immediately following the first World War, two great advances were introduced which improved the efficiency of the Post Office. The first was the development of airmail, which greatly increased the speed with which the mail was delivered. The second was the development of the postage meter machine. It was used for bulk mailing, in which the correct amount of postage was printed for each piece of mail, either directly on the piece or on a label. The Pitney-Bowes company was the largest manufacturer of these machines.

The Great Depression, took its toll on the Post Office, and the years 1930–1934 saw a drop in revenue of almost $119 million dollars. In 1931, the postage stamp was raised from two cents to three cents. Prior to the Depression, the railroads were operated efficiently as the primary transport of the mail, and as the deficits grew larger and larger for them, the department was forced to reduce the number of railroads used to transport the mail. No new motor vehicles were purchased either, and steamship and airline subsidies declined as well. As a result of these operational changes, the Post Office was able to survive the Depression without any serious damage and maintain business as usual.

Author's Note

Babe Ruth actually came to the town of North Adams on August 11, 1938, to play an exhibition game with the Brooklyn Dodgers against the Sons of Italy team. Stan Pasierbiak was the hometown pitcher for the first five innings of the game.

North Adams suffered through three disastrous floods in the twenties and thirties. These occurred in 1927, 1936, and 1938. The Wall Streeter shoe factory was badly flooded in March of 1927, and that is when the workers spent extra time hauling the shoes and equipment out of the flooded factory. It is not clear whether this clean-up was necessary again during the flood of 1936.

FDR actually learned the story he tells Emma in his August 15, 1934, letter about "nother knowledge" at a luncheon at a school dedication in Georgia on May 18, 1937.

Babe Ruth, c. 1920

Yours Truly "Babe" Ruth

© I·L·P

Glossary

Agricultural Adjustment ACT (AAA):
On May 12, 1933, this act was passed to increase farm prices by cutting production and eliminating surplus crops. The government gave farmers direct benefits or rental income if they voluntarily used less acreage for growing crops.

Arthurdale:
In 1933, Eleanor Roosevelt helped establish a planned community in Preston County, West Virginia. It was a model that showed how economically distressed Americans could start supporting themselves on small farms bought on easy credit terms. The people grew their own food while receiving cash income from part-time employment. They built houses out of locally manufactured cinder block and chestnut wood. A school was established, along with a carpentry shop, canning plant, gas station, market, restaurant, and more. On November 20, 1965, Arthurdale became incorporated and was renamed Eleanor in honor of Mrs. Roosevelt.

Civilian Conservation Corps (CCC):
On March 31, 1933, a bill was passed in which 250,000 jobs were created immediately for unemployed men between the ages of eighteen and twenty-five. They lived in camps in the forests and worked planting trees, building roads, and generally improving the land. They received $30 a month with as much as $25 being sent home. By 1941, when it ended, 2 million men had worked in 1,500 CCC camps.

Finishing Tender:
The worker in a textile mill who oversaw the cloth as it was put through a liquid solution and then a drying room to give the material the desired "finish."

Fireside Chats:

President Roosevelt's nationally broadcast radio talks, usually low-key and informal, in which he explained his policies to the American people.

Hobo:

A homeless, penniless beggar who wandered from place to place during the Depression, often hitching free rides on the trains traveling across America.

National Recovery Administration (NRA):

On June 16, 1933, President Roosevelt created this federal agency to establish and administer industrial codes which would regulate wages, hours, and prices for industries. The act also outlawed child labor. Anti-trust laws were suspended and workers were given the right to collective bargaining. The act creating this agency was declared unconstitutional by the Supreme Court in 1935.

National Women's Trade Union League:

Established in November 1903 and originally called the Women's Trade Union League, this was the first national association to organize women workers. It was made up of trade unionists, social reformers, and settlement house workers.

National Youth Administration (NYA):

With this program established on June 25, 1935, grants were given to unmarried students in high school and college in exchange for work.

New Deal:

This was the name given to President Roosevelt's plan between 1933 and 1939 to bring the country out of the Depression. Several of the programs discussed in this book, such as the NRA and the CCC, were established during FDR's first one hundred days in office.

Social Security Act:

Established on August 14, 1935, the Social Security Act set up an old-age pension system so that workers would continue to receive money from the government after they retired. Grants were also provided for financial aid for the handicapped, homeless, dependent children, and others in need.

Tammany Hall:

The executive committee of the Democratic party that ruled New York City from 1850-1933. Although it was tainted with corruption (its leader, Boss William M. Tweed, robbed the city of more than $100 million dollars between 1869 and 1877), it also served the interests of immigrants by finding them jobs and providing them with some form of welfare.

Tennessee Valley Authority (TVA):

Started on May 8, 1933, the TVA was charged with building dams and generating and selling electricity along the Tennessee River. It also developed navigation, maintained flood control, and manufactured and sold fertilizers. Before World War II, six dams were completed.

Wagner Act (also known as National Labor Relations Act):

Established on July 5, 1935, this act stopped employers from interfering with the organization of workers into unions. It defined unfair practices on the part of the employer. Employers were no longer able to fire or otherwise discriminate against those workers who joined a union.

Works Progress Administration (WPA):
Established on April 8, 1935, the WPA employed Americans from all walks of life during the Depression. Workers were hired to build public buildings, airfields, parks, and post offices. Artists painted murals, actors put on plays, and writers conducted interviews with everyday Americans. The government spent $11 billion and employed more than 8 million people in over 1,410,000 projects between 1935 and June 30, 1943.

Interactive Web Footnotes

Here is an alphabetical list of the interactive footnotes found at the bottom of the pages in this book. We hope that this list will prove to be an easy reference for locating the subjects you are interested in at this book's own Web site at **winslowpress.com**.

Index

(Colored numbers represent photographs or illustrated material)

A

B

C

D

Green, William, 48, 72

Groton, 114

H

I

J

L

M

N

O

P

R

T

U

W